Where a dirt road leaves the old Roman road just within the foothills, the Crown Prince Boris of Karlova entered the gloomy precincts of the wood. He rode slowly, as a walk was the only gait possible along the black and winding path.

He had covered perhaps half the distance between the Roman road and Peter's inn when a figure loomed suddenly ahead of him—a tall man, the upper half of his face hidden beneath a black mask, upon a large horse—blocking the way.

"Who the devil are you?" Boris asked.

"I am the Rider," he grinned as he pointed the barrel of his villanous revolver straight at the Prince's breast. . . .

THE RIDER was written in 1915 and published by ALL-STORY WEEKLY in 1918 as "H.R.H. the Rider." In the grand Graustarkian tradition, it involves switched identities and a mysterious highwayman.

This volume was also extra special for Burroughs himself as it was one of the first of 12 ERB books to be illustrated by his younger son, John Coleman Burroughs.

Out of print for over 30 years, THE RIDER is one of the rarest Burroughs works, with copies costing as much as $90. At long last, thanks to Ace Books, fans can inexpensively read this rare work.

Kevin B. Hancer
Columnist for ERB-DOM and GRIDLEY WAVE

EDGAR RICE BURROUGHS

THE RIDER

ace books

A Division of Charter Communications Inc.
1120 Avenue of the Americas
New York, N.Y. 10036

CHAPTER ONE

"I WON'T!" The king tugged upon one end of his grey mustache and frowned upon the speaker.

"I won't!" repeated the Princess Mary, stamping a royal foot in most plebeian anger. "I won't marry a Karlovian. All my life I have been taught to hate Karlova, its ruling house, and its people; and now, just because your stupid old Stroebel wishes it, you tell me that I must marry one of them."

Stroebel, who was standing upon the opposite side of the wide table at which the king sat, smiled indulgently. He loved the Princess Mary—everyone loved her—and he knew that she loved him.

In such a tiny kingdom as Margoth the royal family is not so very far from the people. Instead of being but symbols of power and authority, they are

1

human beings with familiar attributes which render them either very cordially beloved, or very cordially hated, precisely as they may merit.

And Stroebel, already growing grey in the service of his king, was closer to the ruling house than was any other subject. If Stroebel loved the Princess Mary you may rest assured that she deserved it, for grim old Stroebel was not given to loving.

"Your highness must understand," said he, "that while your happiness is close to the hearts of us all, the welfare of Margoth is paramount to all other considerations. Some means must be found to dissipate the ancient enmity which has so long existed between the kingdoms of Margoth and Karlova, that they may combine against the common enemy which threatens them. Both Baron Kantchi and I are agreed that nothing could more satisfactorily produce the desired result than an alliance between the royal houses of Margoth and Karlova."

"And so you and the ambassador from Karlova have decided that I shall be the hollow horned ruminant!" exclaimed the girl, disgustedly.

"The what, Mary?" asked the king.

"The goat," snapped the princess.

The king's frown deepened, but in the eyes of Prince Stroebel there was an unmistakable twinkle.

"I fail to grasp the allusion," said the king, icily; "but I assure that, like your democratic independence, one must need have had an American education to appreciate it. Stroebel!" and the king banged the table top with his clenched fist as he turned upon his prime minister, "it was your importunity which persuaded us against our better judgement to sanction an American education for the Princess Mary. I hope you are satisfied."

Her Royal Highness, the Princess Mary, turned a solemn little face toward Prince Stroebel, and—winked. Then she wheeled toward the king, and taking a quick little step in his direction threw herself into his lap, put her arms about his neck and kissed him.

"Dear old Da-da," she whispered, "don't be cross, please don't; and please, please, please don't make me marry a hideous old Karlovian!"

Through his frown a slow smile touched the lips of the king; but his eyes were sad.

"It is hard to refuse you anything, my child," he said; "but as Prince Stroebel has said, the welfare of Margoth must be first in the hearts of us all. If there are sacrifices to be made, we, to whom God has entrusted the happiness of the people, must be the first to make them. Your childhood has passed, Mary, and now you must be prepared to assume the burdens, yes, and even the sorrows, which your birth entails. Though it fill us with grief we must face the necessity of such an alliance as Prince Stroebel is negotiating."

"But, Da-da," cried the girl, "their faces are a perfect jungle of whiskers, they have bulbous noses, and little, pig eyes. Oh, Da-da, I could never marry a Karlovian prince. I—I'd almost rather be an old maid."

3

"How do you know that the Crown prince of Karlova is so ill-favored?" asked the king. "You have never seen him, or the king, his father."

"I know—Carlotta used to tell me about them," replied the girl. "They were always the ogres in the stories she told me at bedtime, and Carlotta knows— Carlotta knows everything. They eat little girls," and the Princess Mary laughed gaily, though she shuddered a bit, too.

"Carlotta is a dear old fraud," said the king. "She is of the old regime. Times have changed. Now we must love our enemies, or The Great Ogre will eat them and us as well. But, my dear, I will give you this ray of hope—if, when he visits us, Prince Boris of Karlova proves to resemble, even remotely, the ogres of your old nurse's bedtime stories he shall not eat my little girl—no, not if the refusal costs me my throne!"

"He is a gentleman," said Stroebel. "I have it upon the best of authority that he is both affable and well favored."

"He is a Karlovian," cried the Princess Mary, "and I would as lief wed with the devil. When is he coming?"

"Within the month," replied Stroebel.

It was an angry and much perturbed little princess who sought her own apartments when the interview was concluded and confided to her white haired nurse the horror and misery that was in her heart.

"I will not!" she cried for the fortieth time. "I will not marry a Karlovian!"

Not much more than forty-five minutes from Broadway lies the pretentious estate of Abner J. Bass. In one corner, hidden from view by hedges and shrubs, is an old fashioned garden—the especial and particular delight of Miss Gwendolyn Bass, only child and sole heir to the Bass millions.

Buried still further from sight at the far side of the old fashioned garden is a rustic seat, upon which, during a certain lovely afternoon of a June day, a young man sought to hide two dainty little hands within the strong and generous grasp of his own.

"Gwen," he was saying, "I wish to thunder that you were the gardener's daughter, without any incalculable millions looming between us—your father'll never be able to see me as a prospective son-in-law, even with the aid of a magnifying glass."

"Oh," cried the girl, in mock chagrin; "of course, if you prefer the gardener's daughter, there is one; but I rather think she prefers the chauffer. And as to the millions—well, they're mighty nice to have in the family—and you needn't worry about father. He's for anyone I'm for. It's mother you've to persuade—as a loomer mother has the millions beat a city block. You might see mother, Hemmy; but I'm afraid it won't do a bit of good—mother has ideas all her own."

"And if mother refuses?" queried the young man.

The girl raised her shapely shoulders and threw her hands outward, palms up. "If I were a star reporter on a great metropolitan daily," she said, "I should, I think, be more resourceful than your helpless inquiry indicates you to be."

"I suppose that you'd run off with the girl?" he said, laughing.

"That is precisely what I should do," replied Miss Gwendolyn Bass.

"Well, so shall I," he cried.

"With the gardener's daughter, I presume?" asked an acid voice behind them.

The two turned surprised faces in the direction of the speaker. Mr. Hemmington Main rose, rather red of face, and bowed low.

"Mrs. Bass, I'm—I'm mighty sorry," he stammered, "that you chanced to overhear our joking remarks. It was my intention to come to you and Mr. Bass and ask your daughter's hand in a perfectly regular manner. I love——"

The older woman stopped him with uplifted hand. "It is useless, Mr. Main," she said, coldly. "I have other—higher ambitions for my only child. Good afternoon, Mr. Main," and she extended her hand to lay it upon the arm of her daughter. "Come, Gwendolyn!"

It was ten days later that Mr. Hemmington Main received in his morning's mail a letter superscribed in the scrawly and beloved backhand with which he was so familiar—a letter which, after several pages of far greater interest to Mr. Main than to us, ended with: "and so Mother is dragging me off to Europe, ostensibly to forget you; but actually, I am positive, to barter me for a title with a red neck and soiled linen. Father is as mad as I; but helpless. He is for you—horse, foot and artillery—just as I knew he

6

would be. Go and see him—you can weep on one another's shoulder; and in the mean time, Hemmy, take it from me, I'll never, never, never, never marry anybody but you."

And so it was that within that very day Mr. Hemmington Main was ushered into the private office of Abner J. Bass, where the older man greeted his visitor with the kindly smile and the warm handclasp which had been such important factors in the upbuilding of the Bass millions.

"I know why you have called, my boy," he said, without waiting for Mr. Main to explain his mission. "If you hadn't come I should have sent for you—I need your help. Mrs. Bass is, naturally, ambitious for the future of Gwendolyn—so am I; but, unfortunately, in this instance we are not agreed as to what constitutes the elements of a desirable future for our daughter. I could not get away at this time to accompany them abroad—not that I could have accomplished anything had I gone; for Mrs. Bass is, as you know, a very strong character—but I feel that you might accomplish a great deal were you on the spot. Will you go?"

Mr. Hemmington Main was quite taken off his feet by the suddenness of this unexpected proposition— or, it would have been closer to the truth to have said that he was *almost* taken off his feet, for Mr. Main was never quite taken off them in any emergency. And now he was on the point of jumping at this splendid suggestion when there rose before his mind's eye a sordid vision—the same old, squalid specter that had clung so tenaciously to his coat tails and held him into the rut of hard labor since the completion of his college days—Hon. Poverty, with his empty stomach and frayed trousers.

Abner J. Bass noticed the younger man's hesitation, and he guessed its cause.

"You won't have to worry about the financial end of the undertaking," he said. "I'll see to that."

"But I couldn't go that way, sir," expostulated Mr. Main. "Can't you see that I couldn't do it?"

"No, I can't see anything of the sort," replied Mr. Bass. "If my money is going to be used to buy a husband for Gwendolyn, I am going to see that it buys a husband she wants; and if you love her half as much as she deserves you won't let pride stand in the way of her happiness. Don't be foolish, Main; we've got to work together, each giving what he has to give—you, youth, vigor and resourcefulness; I, financial backing," and without waiting for a reply the older man wheeled about to his desk, opened a check book and filled in a blank check.

"Here," he said, extending the bit of paper toward Hemmington Main, "take this for preliminary expenses, and then draw on me for as much more as you may need, when you need it—I'll make the necessary arrangements through our London office. Now run along, and get busy."

CHAPTER TWO

PRINCE BORIS of Karlova stood at attention in the presence of his august sire. The latter was large and red of neck, bullet headed and heavy jowled. He hammered his desk with a huge fist, the while he roared his denunciation in stentorian tones.

"You are better fitted for a court jester than a crown prince," he shouted. "Your escapades are the gossip of the capitol. Scullery maids and hostlers know you better than do the nobility of the unhappy kingdom which some day will be forced to acknowledge you its king. You are a disgrace to the royal blood of the house of Kargovitch. You—you—you——"

"Otherwise," interrupted the crown prince, "I am everything which your majesty could desire."

The face of King Constans of Karlova turned from red to purple, he half rose from his chair and beat upon the desk with two fists instead of one.

"Enough of your impudence!" he cried. "You are under arrest, sir! Go to your quarters, and remain there—indefinitely."

"Yes, Sire," replied Prince Boris; "but I suggest that you place a guard over me, as I have not given you my parole. Confinement is irksome to me—I shall escape, if I can; and then there is no telling but that I may marry a scullery maid and infuse into the veins of the Kargovitches a few ounces of red blood."

"Your marriage already is arranged," roared the king. "It was upon that subject I wished to speak with you—your impudence drove it from my mind. You will wed the Princess Mary of Margoth—if she will have you; and you will remain under arrest until Baron Kantchi has arranged the time of your visit to the court of Margoth."

The young man took a step toward his father.

"But, your majesty," he exclaimed, "I do not wish to marry yet—and above all others I do not wish to marry a Margoth princess, who, unquestionably has a scrawny neck and the temper of a termagant."

"It is immaterial whether she has any neck or any temper," replied the king; "you are going to marry her; and I trust that she will be able to accomplish what I have failed to—the awakening in you a realization of the obligations of your exalted birth."

"I hope so," said the crown prince aloud; but what he thought is not recordable.

The king touched a bell upon his desk, and an instant later an officer of the guard entered the apartment and bowed low before his sovereign.

"You will conduct Prince Boris to his quarters," said Constans. "He is under arrest. Place a guard over him, as he has refused us his parole."

The officer bowed again, and backed from the presence, followed by the crown prince.

In silence the two traversed the corridors of the palace until they came to the apartments of Prince Boris. A soldier, already on guard there, saluted as the two passed within; and a moment later the officer emerged and transmitted to the sentry the orders of the king.

Within the apartment Boris glanced at his watch. A smile touched his lips. "An hour," he murmured, "—I can barely make it."

He approached the door and opened it. The sentry saluted, stiff and rigid. The crown prince examined the man's features—he did not recognize them. The man was a recruit in the palace guard. Boris sighed. A veteran might have been easier to handle, for the veterans all loved the crown prince.

"My man," said Boris, "if you will just cast your eyes in the other direction for a moment you will not see me escape—and what people don't see, you know, won't ever do them any harm."

The sentry wheeled about and faced the crown prince, barring the doorway with his rifle.

"I am sorry, your highness," he said respectfully;

"but I cannot do it—I cannot violate the oath I took when I was sworn into the king's service."

"Quite right," exclaimed Boris. "I am glad to hear you say that—it goes to prove that you are a loyal fellow. I saw that you were new in the service and I wished to test you—you did well to refuse."

He turned to re-enter the room, but as he was about to close the door after him he paused and cast a quick glance over his shoulder at the sentry.

"You have never before stood guard before may apartment?" he asked.

"Never, your highness," replied the soldier.

"And your sergeant told you nothing about my nightmares?" continued the prince.

"Nothing, your highness."

"He should have," commented Boris. "He should have instructed you that I am subject to nightmares, and that when you hear me moaning or crying out in my sleep you should come in at once and awaken me."

"But your highness's valet sleeps in the adjoining apartment," suggested the soldier; "—he will awaken you."

"He sleeps like a dead man," replied Boris. "Nothing awakens him. If you hear me, come in at once and awaken me—do you understand?"

"Yes, your highness," and the soldier saluted again.

"Good-night," said the prince, "and lose no time when you hear me—I usually have them early in the night, when I first fall asleep."

"Good-night, your highness," replied the sentry. "I will come if I hear you."

For a few minutes Prince Boris moved about his apartment, talking in low tones to his valet; but he did not remove his clothes. Presently he dismissed the man, turned out his lights and clambered into bed with all his clothes on. A broad smile illumined his countenance, and it was with difficulty that he repressed a chuckle.

Beyond the door the sentry stood in statuesque rigidity in the corridor. The great clock at the far end of the passageway ticked out the seconds. Slowly the minutes passed. Silence reigned in this part of the palace, though it was still early in the evening.

Presently the sentry cocked an attentive ear— instantly alert. An unmistakable moan had issued from the apartment of the crown prince. It was immediately followed by a smothered wail. The sentry wheeled, turned the knob and entered the apartment. As he crossed quickly toward the bed where Prince Boris lay his back was toward the doorway leading into the adjoining apartment where the prince's valet was supposed to be sleeping like a dead man, and so the sentry did not see the dark robed figure which glided into the bed chamber of the prince and followed him to the royal bed-side.

Another moan came from the tossing figure upon the bed. The sentry leaned over and shook the sleeper by the shoulder; and as he did so the bed clothes rose suddenly and enveloped his head, a pair of strong arms encircled his neck about the bed clothes and another pair of arms seized him from behind.

A moment later he lay bound and gagged upon the bed recently occupied by Prince Boris of Karlova. A dark robed figure glided silently from the apartment, and the crown prince touched a button which flooded the room with light. The sentry looked up into the smiling face of his captor.

"Awfully sorry, my man," said Prince Boris; "but I have a very important engagement for this evening— see you later. Hope you find my bed comfortable; and whatever you do don't have a nightmare, for my man is a very heavy sleeper—just like a dead man, you know," and Boris of Karlova slipped a light cloak over his shoulders and passed out into the corridor before his apartments.

Ten minutes later a solitary horseman rode slowly through the darker streets of the capitol and out of the city by the long unguarded west gate. Once in the country he put spurs to his mount and rode at a sharp trot along the wide, grey pike.

CHAPTER THREE

KARLOVA is a mountainous little kingdom. Sovgrad, its capitol city, lies in a fertile little hollow surrounded by many hills through which the old Roman road winds in an easterly direction toward the frontier and Margoth. Just beyond the shoulder of the first of the low foot hills a dirt road diverges northward from the main highway, and passing beneath overhanging trees wriggles to and fro through a grim and forbidding forest. Five or six miles above the Roman road it skirts a royal hunting preserve, the favorite abode of Prince Boris. Scarce a quarter of a mile within the wood and a hundred yards back from the dirt road lies an old inn—a place of none too savory reputation, where questionable characters from the city of Sovgrad were reputed to meet and concoct their deviltries against the majesty of the law.

Here too were wont to forgather a little coterie of another class—a half dozen young sprigs of the ancient nobility of Karlova, lured by the spirit of romance and adventure to this haunt of the lower world, and enticed by the cookery of the inn keeper's wife and the vintages of the black cellars to numerous repetitions of their original excursion, until now they had become regular patrons of the establishment.

Tonight three of them sat at a round table in a tiny alcove, sipping their wine and venturing various explanations of the lateness of one whose empty chair broke the circle at the little board.

There was Alexander Palensk, whose father is prime minister of Karlova, and Nicholas Gregovitch, the son of General Demitrius Gregovitch, minister of war. The third, Ivan Kantchi, is the oldest son of the Karlovian ambassador to Margoth, and all three are officers in The Black Guard—the crack regiment of the Karlovian army.

The fourth member of the party—he whose chair still remained vacant—was riding at a rapid trot along the Roman road as Ivan Kantchi asked, for the fortieth time: "What could have delayed him? Why the devil doesn't he come?"

"Calm thyself, Little One," admonished Alexander Palensk, with an affectionate smile at the giant Ivan, whose six-foot-six had won him the loving diminutive; "our brother is doubtless afraid to ride after dark. The wood is gloomy, and, as is well known, infested by goblins. Chances are that he turned back before quitting the Roman road and has fled home to his nurses's arms."

"Screaming in terror," added Nicholas Gregovitch, whereupon all three fell to laughing; but beneath his levity, Ivan Kantchi was still worried.

"You know," he said, after a moment's silence, "that The Rider is reputed to have been seen in this neighborhood quite recently. There have been no less than three highway robberies on the Roman road within the month, and all perpetrated by a lone horseman who answers the description of the fellow who has worked the southern provinces for the past three or four years. I think I shall ride toward the city and have a look for our friend."

"Oh, sit down, Little One," cried Alexander, "and let us finish this bottle in peace—if he has not come by then we will all ride forth and rescue him from the clutches of The Rider or the goblins, whichever has abducted our tender little playmate."

Ivan dropped back into his chair. "It is unfortunate," he said, "that Prime Ministers couldn't bequeath a little more brain power to their offspring."

"*Gesundheit!*" cried Alexander, raising his glass and grinning good naturedly at his friend.

Where the dirt road leaves the Roman road just within the foothills a horseman reined his mount to the left and entered the dark and gloomy precincts of the wood. He rode slowly, letting his beast pick its own way, since he could scarce see his own hand before his face. Gradually his eyes became accustomed to the darkness, but yet a walk was the only gait possible along the black and winding road.

He had covered perhaps half the distance between the Roman road and the inn when a figure loomed suddenly ahead of him—a tall man upon a large horse—blocking the way. Even in the dark the rider could see the glint of reflected light upon the barrel of a long revolver which was levelled straight at his breast.

"Hold up your hands!" whispered the stranger.

The rider did as he was bid. The other slid from his saddle and approached him. Deft fingers felt over his person in search of weapons, of which the rider carried none.

"Dismount!" commanded the stranger.

The victim lowered his hands to the pommel of his saddle.

"Who the devil are you?" he asked. "Is it that I have the honor of addressing The Rider?" The tone was mocking.

"Get down, or you'll get hurt," replied the highwayman surlily. "I am The Rider, and if you know anything of me you must know that I don't put up with any trifling."

Through the darkness the rider grinned down upon the man who held his bridle rein and covered him with a long and villainous looking revolver.

" 'The Rider,' " he repeated. "A name to conjure with!"

"Get down, you fool," growled the highwayman.

" 'The Rider'!" continued the horseman, ignoring the other's command. "How envious my friends will be when I tell them that I have indeed been waylaid by that notorious, nay, let us say, famous gentleman of the road. But will they believe me? They will think me but an idle boaster—unless I take some token of the adventure——"

"Enough, idiot!" cried The Rider, releasing the bridle rein and stepping forward to seize the horseman and drag him from his saddle. "Do you think that I have all night and the next day to trifle with a second groom or a grocer's clerk, who doubtless won't yield the price of a bottle of stale beer?"

He seized his victim's arm roughly to unhorse him, and at the same instant the latter lunged forward upon the bandit, carrying him heavily to the ground, flat upon his back. Long, powerful fingers closed upon The Rider's pistol wrist, while, with his right hand, the horseman found the other's throat.

Futilely the brigand kicked, struggled and struck. His right hand was numbing in the steel grip that held him vise-like—his revolver was useless. The fingers at his throat were shutting off his breath, so that to his first anger and chagrin was now added a real terror for his life.

"No," said the man upon his chest, "they never will believe me, unless I take with me some token of this delightful meeting—and what evidence more conclusive than the person of The Rider himself! Ah, just the thing, my dear fellow! You shall accompany me! In the flesh and blood, and by the word of your own mouth shall you attest to the truth of the fact that I was waylaid, in the dead of night, upon a lonely road by none other and none less than the redoubtable and uncapturable Rider."

As he finished speaking he tightened his grip upon The Rider's wrist until the unhappy man thought that the bones must splinter beneath those steel fingers. At the same time the pressure at his throat was lessened.

"Lay aside your weapon, my friend," admonished the cheerful voice above him; "Lay it aside lest you harm yourself with so dangerous a plaything."

The revolver slipped from the relaxing fingers of the bandit.

"Thank you," said the voice.

The hand left The Rider's throat, and felt over his person for other weapons. Finding none, it reached out and gathered in the revolver which The Rider had just relinquished, then the weight was removed from the bandit's chest as the other rose and stood beside him.

"Come, get up!" cried the victor. "My, but you are a slothful fellow!"

The Rider scrambled to his feet, and faced his conqueror.

"Who the devil are you?" he cried.

"I might be a hostler," replied the other; "but a grocer's clerk—never! Now that I have a revolver, I could borrow your mask and set up in business as a brigand, eh? What sort of highwayman do you think I'd make, my friend?"

The Rider mumbled an unintelligible reply. His pride had been sorely lacerated and he was in no very good humor.

"Come on, sunshine," cried his captor, "let us mount and seek my friends," and he motioned The Rider toward the latter's horse which stood where the bandit had left it in the middle of the road.

Here the captor removed a second revolver from a saddle holster, slipped it inside his shirt, and swung into his own saddle as The Rider mounted.

"Where are you going to take me?" asked the crestfallen brigand.

"To the inn of that old rogue, Peter, where my friends are waiting for me this two hours."

A smile curved the lips of The Rider. Peter's Inn! More than one of The Rider's friends would be there, too.

"And there you will vouch for my story, eh, Sunshine? that I was stopped upon the highroad by none other than the great Rider."

As the two rode on in the direction of the inn The Rider's captor kept up a good natured raillery at the expense of the bandit, while the latter, still aggrieved, answered only in monosyllables when a question was put to him and bided his time against their arrival at the place where he was sure he would find enough of his followers to insure escape, as well as punishment for this presumptious hostler who had dared to turn the tables upon the terror of the highways.

CHAPTER FOUR

AT THE inn, Alexander, Nicholas, and Ivan had finished their wine and were preparing to take their departure in search of their missing friend. A dozen or more rough and unkempt fellows were drinking in the open bar room and mine host Peter, together with trig little Bakla, was bustling about wiping off table tops, removing empty mugs and glasses, and replacing them with filled ones.

In the smoke begrimed kitchen adjoining the bar Peter's frowzy fraw broiled with her steaks before a glowing grill. From the pipe between her toothless gums to the dirt upon her bare feet she was all athrob with the ecstacy of a true artist, for tonight she was preparing a dinner for the fine young gentlemen from the capitol, who could appreciate such

23

culinary achievements as her's. The swine she ordinarily cooked for knew nothing of the divine exquisiteness of the food she served them, yet, being a true artist who labors first for the love of art, Peter's frau cooked as well for them as for the more appreciative, though with scarce the same enthusiasm.

Upon her artistic reveries now broke Bakla, with a rude interruption. The gentlemen were leaving. They had sent word that they would return when they had located their missing friend. Tillie threw up her hands in horror. The dinner would be spoiled! In fifteen minutes it would be ready to serve. She rushed toward the doorway leading into the barroom. She would explain. She would entreat the fine, young gentlemen to eat first and seek their friend later. Bakla trotted in the wake of her mistress. She, too, was perturbed; but not on account of the spoiled dinner. Bakla shared the uneasiness of the departing guests over the unaccountable tardiness of the missing friend—the tall, black haired, grey-eyed young man who smiled much and spoke always in a soft and kindly voice. He had been coming here to Peter's Inn for many months, and though she did not know who he might be she was convinced that he was a very fine gentleman with a great deal of money and a large and generous heart. Many were the sighs that Bakla had heaved to the heroic figure of this guest of guests.

As Tillie and Bakla rushed into the bar-room the three young gentlemen were just slipping on their military capes as they crossed the sanded floor toward the doorway at the opposite side of the room.

At the same moment the door swung open and a tall figure, booted and spurred, filled the doorway. The upper half of his face was hidden beneath a black mask. The three departing guests halted in the middle of the floor, and three hands flew to the hilts of three swords. The man at the doorway stepped within, disclosing another, equally as tall, directly behind him. At the sight of the face of the latter, Ivan gave voice to an exclamation of relief.

"Dimmie!" he cried. "It's Dimmie! Where have you been? We were just setting out to look for you, and who the devil have you with you?"

Dimmie stepped into the room and bowed low to his friends and the assembled guests, servants, and hosts of Peter's Inn.

"Permit me," he said, "to present my very good friend The Rider!"

A chorus of exclamations greeted the introduction. The roughs rose from their tables and pressed forward, as did the three guardsmen, Peter, Tillie, and Bakla.

"The Rider!" exclaimed Bakla, clasping her little hands together in an ecstacy of thrills.

"He held me up upon the road, Alexander," cried Dimmie. "I knew you would never believe me unless I brought proof, and so I persuaded my good friend to come along with me and assure you that it is indeed true that I have been waylaid by no less a person than the much talked of Rider. Eh, Sunshine, is it not true?" and the speaker turned toward his captive.

A surly looking fellow who had been sitting alone at a far table now shouldered his way through the crowd about the two new comers. His evil, little eyes scanned the faces of them both; and it is a matter open to dispute as to which of the figures caused him the greater astonishment.

The Rider saw him and hung his head. Then he looked up, caught the other's eye, and surreptitiously touched the empty holster at his hip. The other raised his eyebrows in mingled surprise and understanding.

Ivan was also examining the two men. He noted that he of the mask was unarmed, while Dimmie carried a long, evil looking revolver half hidden behind him. Suddenly he burst into a loud laugh.

Alexander and Nicholas looked at him in surprise. The Rider glanced quickly over the faces of the assembled guests. Fully half were men of his own stamp with whom he was familiar in the vice haunts of the city; but only one, he of the small and evil eyes, knew that their city crony and The Rider were one and the same.

Suddenly the bandit snatched the mask from his face, revealing a countenance wherein intelligence and bestiality were oddly combined. The forehead was high and broad, the ears well set, but a trifle too small, the chin and mouth sensitive without weakness. The man's nose and eyes were the least prepossessing of his features. The former was slightly bulbous, while the latter were small and close-set.

At sight of The Rider's face a number of the rougher guests gave vent to expressions of astonished recognition, and exclamations of, "The Wolf," fell from the lips of several.

"Yes," said The Rider, "I am The Wolf, your old friend and comrade. Will you see me dragged off to prison by a handful of dandies—me, who could send the half of you to the halter if I chose?"

"That we'll not," growled one of the drinkers. "Come, comrades, pluck these fine chickens and throw them out to the dogs. We do not want them here. Peter's place belongs to us. What business have they here? Come!" and he stepped truculently forward toward him whom Ivan had addressed as Dimmie.

Tillie, a large grilling fork in one huge, red hand, ran screaming toward the speaker.

"Pig!" she cried, "what would you do? Chase away the only guests who have brains enough to know what they are putting into their stomachs and purses long enough to pay for what they eat and drink and I'll have the rotten heart out of you!"

But the man was already beside Dimmie. One paw-like hand was clutching for the young man's shoulder. Alexander, Nicholas, and Ivan sprang forward with cries of mingled rage and horrified warning. The Rider, seeing his opportunity, also turned upon his captor; but Dimmie, still smiling good naturedly, let drive a smashing right that caught the would be deliverer of The Rider full in the mouth and sent him sprawling backward upon the floor. Then he wheeled upon The Rider just as the latter seized him about the body, reached quickly over his shoulders, caught him around the waist, and, lifting him bodily from the floor, hurled him completely over his head.

In the mean time the three guardsmen were engaged with others of the roughs who had entered the fracas in the defense of their friends. No weapons had been drawn upon either side—as yet it was but a rough and tumble fist fight. The revolver which Dimmie had held when he entered the room he had slipped inside his shirt with its fellow, and now that he had disposed temporarily of the two who had attacked him he ran to the assistance of his friends.

Ivan and Nicholas were holding their own with ease; but three men had engaged Alexander at once, and he was in a fair way to being beaten into insensibility when Dimmie leaped upon the back of one of his adversaries, hurled him aside, and struck another a blow upon the chin that might have dropped a horse. As the third attempted to scramble from his path, the young man swung his foot in a kick that sent the fellow sprawling beneath a table.

Tillie, appalled by the dimensions and ferocity of the fracas, had retreated to the side of the room, where she stood with Bakla and the trembling Peter, wringing her hands and screaming out a torrent of invective. Beside her and next to Bakla stood the surly rough who had been the first to recognize The Rider. He had taken no part in the fight, and now one of his friends discovered him, and taunted him with his seeming cowardice.

The man muttered an oath, and turning to Bakla, said: "If the fools knew who they were fighting with they'd break all your windows trying to see which could get out of here first and lose himself in the woods."

"What do you mean?" asked Bakla. "Can they not see that they are attacking officers of The Black Guard?"

"I don't mean them fellows," growled the man. "It's the other—do you mean to say you don't none of you know who he is?"

"Why of course I know who he is," cried the girl. "He has been coming here for months—he is M. Dimmie."

"M. Dimmie, hell," cried the man. "That's—," and he leaned close to Bakla's ear and whispered a name that brought her eyes and mouth open in incredulous astonishment.

The fight seemed to be going all the guardsmen's way, when The Rider bolted suddenly for the door. Dimmie sprang across a table in a mad effort to head off the escaping bandit, and the two met before the exit. Once again The Rider went down before the superior skill of his antagonist; and Dimmie turned with his back to the doorway as Alexander, Ivan, and Nicholas ran to his side.

A laugh was on the lips of the conqueror of the redoubtable highwayman as the latter crawled to his feet, nursing a bloody nose with one hand, and, turning to his friends, who were now grouped in sullen defiance before the bar, called to them to rush the four at the doorway and make good their escape.

"I was afraid the fun was over, Ivan," said Dimmie; "but evidently it has only begun."

"Come!" whispered Alexander, in his ear. "The door is behind us—let's get out of here before any blood is spilled. The thing has gone far enough. These fellows are getting nasty, and there is no telling what may happen—there are more than a few knives and revolvers in that crowd."

"Never!" cried Dimmie. "I am having the time of my life, old killjoy; and I'm going to stick for the finish. Run, if you want to—the door is there, and we will cover your retreat."

Alexander flushed. "You know that I would not desert you," he cried. "I only thought of the danger to your——"

"Sh-sh-sh!" admonished Dimmie with a gesture of arrogance. "Forget it!"

The roughs were advancing slowly across the barroom, when one of them passing a table which had not been overturned in the previous scrimmage, seized an empty bottle and hurled it viciously at the four guardsmen. It grazed Dimmie's head and splintered on the oak panel behind him. Instantly Alexander leaped in front of his friend, and drew his sword.

"Stop!" he cried. "This has gone far enough. In the king's name, I command you to halt where you are!"

The answer to his order was a volley of glasses and bottles. Ivan seized a small table and raised it as a

shield before them. Nicholas drew his sword and
took his place on one side of the improvised barrier,
while Alexander held the other.

At sight of the drawn weapons the crowd of cut-
throats and thieves cast discretion to the winds.
Knives flashed, and revolvers flourished. A sullen
roar rose from the pack.

Dimmie, the inextinguishable smile still upon his
lips, thrust aside his protectors, and stepped out before the menacing foe, one hand upraised for silence
and attention.

"Hold, my friends," he said "We have enjoyed a
pleasant evening. None more so than I. Let us not
spoil it now by the spilling of blood."

As he spoke a man stepped forward from the
crowd advancing from the bar. A revolver glistened
in his hand. Blood streamed down his brutal face
from a wound above one eye. Behind him, unnoticed
came Bakla.

"You have come here once too often, you dandies,"
cried the fellow. "You have come looking for trouble;
and now you've got it, and damn you you're goin' to
get it good and plenty," and with that he raised his
weapon and levelled it at Dimmie.

Ivan cast the table aside, and he and Alexander
and Nicholas sprang forward to throw themselves in
front of their friend, to shield his body with their
own from the bullet of the assassin; but trig little
Bakla was quicker than any of them. Without a cry
she leaped at the man as his finger closed downward
upon the trigger. Her lithe figure dodged beneath his

upraised arm, which she clutched with both her little hands. There was the sharp report of a shot; but the bullet buried itself in the ceiling instead of finding lodgement in the body of Dimmie for whom it had been intended.

Bakla, still clinging to the man's arm, threw herself in front of him and facing the menacing roughs, raised her voice in protest and in censure.

"Are you crazy," she cried, "that you would fit halters to your necks by threatening the life of the king's son?"

"The what?" exclaimed the man whose arm she still held raised aloft.

"The Crown Prince, you fool," snapped Bakla.

The man gazed stupidly at the three guardsmen and their friend, only the last of which was not in uniform.

"Which is the Crown Prince?" he asked.

"He," and she pointed at Dimmie. "He is Prince Boris."

The roughs looked uneasily around at one another. One of them laughed scornfully. "That the crown prince?" he asked with a sneer.

"Yes," spoke up he of the low brow and surly expression who had kept carefully out of the fracas from the moment that he had recognized Dimmie; "he's Prince Boris. I ought to know him—I worked in the palace for five years."

An uneasy silence fell upon the company. Those who had menaced the prince shuffled their feet about on the sanded floor and cast furtive glances in the direction of their future king, who stood, unsmiling now and rather ill at ease since his identity had been revealed.

"I think we'd better go now," suggested Alexander. "The thing has gone too far already; and the longer we stay the worse it may become—you'll have a bad enough time explaining it to his majesty as it is, Dimmie."

"Without our dinner?" asked Boris, ruefully. "No, I came for one of Tillie's good dinners; and I'll never leave until I've had it. Here, Peter, you old rogue, see what the gentlemen will drink," and he waved his hand to include the whole company, "and Bakla, lay another plate at our table for my guest, if The Rider will honor us with his company?" and he turned with a bow toward the bandit.

"And then go back to Sovgrad and the halter?" demanded The Rider.

Boris drew the man's two revolvers from his shirt and extended them toward him, butts first.

"Here are your weapons," he said, pleasantly. "Take them as proof of my good faith. After we have dined each of us shall go his way unmolested, carrying only memories of a pleasant evening among friends. What do you say?"

"Done!" said The Rider.

The king's son linked arms with the bandit and crossed the room past the bar where Peter was already busy serving drinks to the relieved brawlers, toward the little alcove in which Bakla was laying the fifth plate at the round table.

"You must have had many thrilling adventures," said Boris to his guest, after the dinner and the wine had warmed the latter's heart and loosed his naturally taciturn tongue. "Tell us of them."

For an hour The Rider told them tales of the road —of narrow escapes, of running fights with gendarmes, of rich hauls, and of lean days. When he paused to light another of Ivan's gold tipped and monogrammed cigarets, Boris leaned back in his chair with a deep sigh.

"Ah," he murmured, "such freedom! You have lived. For such as you romance still exists; but for us life is a tame and prosaic thing. I wish that I were a bandit."

"And I," said The Rider, "wish that I were a prince."

Boris sat suddenly erect with a half smothered exclamation.

"Why not!" he cried. It would be great sport.

"Why not what?" asked Nicholas.

"Be a bandit for a week," replied Boris.

The others leaned back in their chairs, shouting in laughter. Ivan, tying a napkin about the lower half of his face, rose and pointed a salt shaker at Alexander, menacingly.

"Stand and deliver!" he cried. "I am Dimmie, the terror of the highways."

Boris joined in the good natured raillery; but when the laughter had subsided he turned toward The Rider.

"You have said that you would like being a prince,"

he said. "Well, you shall be, for a week, and I shall borrow your horse and your mask and uphold the honor of your calling upon the roads."

"Dimmie, you're crazy," cried Alexander, realizing at last that Boris was in earnest.

The crown prince paid no attention to his friend's interruption.

"And you," he continued, still addressing the bandit, "shall live like a prince while I am gone."

"It can't be done, Dimmie," broke in Alexander. "How could this man pass as Prince Boris? Except in size you are as unlike as two men can be. Where could he go to play prince where the imposture would not be immediately discovered and exposed?"

"My hunting lodge," cried Boris. "It's just the place."

"But, Dimmie," expostulated Ivan, "within the week you will receive his majesty's commands to proceed to Demia, for the purpose of paying court to the future crown princess of Karlova—I have had the information in a letter from my father."

"Good!" exclaimed Boris. "Now I am unalterably decided, and a setting is provided where our friend here may play prince to his heart's content and do me a good turn into the bargain."

"What do you mean?" asked Nicholas.

"I mean," replied Boris, "that I shall send The Rider to Demia to pay court to the Princess Mary of Margoth.

The three guardsmen gasped.

"You are my best friends," continued Boris. "A

thousand times have you sworn that you would willingly lay down your lives for me. Now I shall discover how sincere were your protestations of fidelity. I do not wish to marry, yet; and most certainly I do not wish to marry a scrawny-necked, watery-eyed Margoth princess. If she refuses me, I shall be saved; and our friend here can see to it that she refuses. Should she accept him," and Boris could not restrain a grin of amusement, "I shall still be saved, since she will be married to another."

"But Dimmie," cried Alexander, seriously, "you cannot mean to carry your hoax as far as that! It would mean war, Dimmie."

"And which of you would not prefer war with Margoth?" asked Boris.

The others were silent. Prince Boris had spoken the truth, for the military party of Karlova had for long sought to foment trouble between the two countries. The crown prince, to whom they looked for guidance, had counselled temperance, and though the acknowledged head of the war party he had been the strongest advocate of peace with Margoth. Now, however, that a distasteful marriage was to be thrust upon him he was quite willing to go to any lengths, though the principal appeal of the adventure lay in its levity.

CHAPTER FIVE

THE city of Demia was draped with bunting. The flags of Karlova and Margoth floated from a thousand windows and balconies. They were suspended across the main thoroughfares upon ropes of flowers. The colors of Karlova were twined with those of Margoth upon the coats of the men of Margoth and in the dark hair of the women; yet, notwithstanding these outward symbols of rejoicing, the hearts of the Margothians were heavy, for today a Karlovian prince was coming to pay court to their beloved princess, Mary of Margoth.

In the palace of the king the object of their devotion stamped back and forth the length of her boudoir. Her little hands were flying in excited gestures as she stormed vehemently to the sympathetic ear of her audience of one. Faithful Carlotta shared her mistress's aversion to the thought of the impending calamity.

"I won't! I won't! I won't!" cried Mary. "I'll —I'll die first. I won't marry a hideous, hateful Karlovian. I don't care if I am a princess. It isn't my fault; and I don't want to be one, anyway."

"My dear child," and Carlotta's voice was choked with sobs; "if poor old Carlotta could only help you! But there is no help. You were born to the purple, and you must accept the responsibilities of the purple; and, too, dear, you may find that Prince Boris is not entirely impossible—even though he be a Karlovian. He——"

"Carlotta!" interrupted the Princess Mary, clapping her palms together. "I have it!"

"Have what?" asked Carlotta.

"Never mind what I have; but I have it; and, Carlotta, pay no attention to anything that I may say or do while Prince Boris is present. Do you understand?"

There was a blare of trumpets from far down the broad avenue which leads up to the palace.

"He is coming!" cried Carlotta.

"But he won't stay long," said Princess Mary, with a shrug and a girlish giggle.

In the uniform of colonel of The Black Guard, and attended only by three officers of that famous regiment, came Boris, Prince of Karlova to the court of Alexis III. Between lines of royal troops, down a flower-strewn boulevard he rode in the French limousine which had brought him along the Roman road from Sovgrad to Demia. Prince Stroebel, Prime Minister of Margoth had met him at the city gates, and now sat beside him. The crown prince of Karlova seemed ill at ease. He played with the sword knot upon the hilt of the jeweled weapon at his side. He cast apprehensive glances at the long line of soldiery, standing with arms at the present along either hand. To the perfunctory plaudits of the citizens of Demia he made no response.

Ivan Kantchi, who sat just in front of him, kicked his royal foot and made a surreptitious gesture toward his helmet. The crown prince snatched off his own headgear and waved it frantically at the cheering populace. Ivan Kantchi bit his lip, and a slow flush crept up from beneath his military collar. Prince Stroebel became acutely interested in something straight ahead of him. Alexander Palensk, sitting beside Ivan, gave the latter an almost imperceptible nudge with his elbow. The people packing either side of the avenue gazed wide eyed at the crown prince of Karlova for a moment; then they broke into loud and tumultuous laughter.

Prince Boris glanced nervously to right and left. He saw the strained expressions upon the faces of his companions, he sensed the jeers in the laughter of the people of Demia. Then he lost his temper. Jamming his helmet down upon his head, the eagles of The Black Guard to the rear instead of in front, he rose to his feet, and shaking his fists at the Margothians unloosed a stream of profane invective upon them.

A young American, standing upon a balcony of Demia's principal hotel, witnessed the outbreak.

"The future husband of your princess appears to have a little temper of his own," he commented, grinning, to a chance acquaintance at his side. The latter, a very tall young man, broad shouldered and with an unmistakably military bearing, smiled.

"He doesn't seem to be making a very good impression, does he?" he asked. "But you are mistaken, M. Main, in thinking me a Margothian. I am not. Just a chance visitor to Demia, like yourself."

"Well," said Hemmington Main, "I hope that whatever your business here may be that you are more successful than I have been. One disappointment after another has been my lot since I first reached Europe, and now I have entirely lost track of those I am seeking. They should have arrived in Demia three days since, and I can only account for their absence on the hypothesis that—ahem—one of them discovered that I was following them and has altered their route in order to elude me."

"You are an American detective?" asked the stranger.

Main laughed. "Far from it," he replied; "though I have often thought, until recently, that I was a natural born sleuth; and now to lose two women and a chauffeur, to say nothing of two maids and an automobile, in the heart of Europe is a severe blow to my egotism."

"My dear fellow," exclaimed the stranger; "can it be that be that you are trailing a convent?"

"I'm trailing the dearest girl in the world," replied Main.

The other raised his eyebrows in partial understanding.

"Ah," he said; "a love affair—romance—adventure! My dear M. Main, I think that you are a man after my own heart, with this slight difference—you are seeking to find a love, I to elude one. Possibly we might join forces, eh?"

"How?"

"I do not know—we must leave that to fate; and while fate is mustering her forces let us find a table here on the balcony and investigate again that incomparable 'bronx' which you taught the bar boy to concoct before we were interrupted by the coming of His Royal Highness, Prince Boris of Karlova."

"You're on," cried Hemmington Main. "His royal nibs has passed. The troops are going. Hoi polloi are dispersing. The circus parade is over—now for red lemonade and peanuts."

"You Americans don't entertain a great deal of respect for royalty," commented the stranger, with a good natured laugh.

"Oh, but we do," replied Main. "We deride the gods even while we tremble at their feet. We poke fun at kings, for whose lightest favor we would barter our souls. We are a strange race, monsieur. Europeans do not know us; nor is it strange, for, as a matter of fact, we do not know ourselves."

The two men had seated themselves at a small table near the balustrade, overlooking the avenue beneath. Traffic was once more assuming its normal condition, though many pedestrians still lingered in idle gossip upon the narrow walks. An automobile, a large touring car, honked noisily out of a side street and crossed toward the hotel entrance. Main chanced to be looking down into the street at the time. With an excited exclamation he half rose from his chair.

"There they are!" he whispered. "There she is, now."

"Who?" asked the stranger.

"The convent," explained Main.

"Good! You are something of a detective, after all."

The car drew up before the hotel and stopped. Two maids alighted, followed by a young girl and a white haired woman.

"I am interested, my friend," said the stranger. "Tell me something of your romance—it is possible that I may be of assistance to you."

Main looked the other squarely in the eyes. He had been attracted to the man from the first by that indefinable something which inspires confidence and belief even in total strangers.

"My dear Kargovitch," he said, "I do not know you from the side of a barn; but I like you. You are what my friend Garrigan of the late Chicago Press Club would call 'a regular fellow.' I think I'll tell you my troubles; but I'll promise not to weep on your shoulder—the bronx is far too mild for that."

M. Kargovitch leaned across the table and laid a hand on the American's shoulder.

"I am glad that you like me, my friend," he said; "and I can assure you that I return the compliment. Tell me no more than you care to; and if I can help you, I will.

Hemmington Main let his eyes return from the walk below, from which the little party had disappeared from the automobile into the interior of the hotel.

"It is this way," he said. "The young lady whom you just saw leaving the machine is Miss Gwendolyn Bass, daughter of Abner J. Bass the multi-millionaire American. I—er—ah—we, well, you understand; she is perfectly willing to become Mrs. Hemmington Main; and her father is with us, strong; but Mamma Bass has aspirations. She wants a title in the family. Money, of course, is no object to them. The fact that I am poor means nothing to Mrs. Bass one way or another; but, you see, being a plain American, I am absolutely titleless and, therefore, impossible. Gwendolyn would marry me in a minute if we could get her away from her mother long enough to have the ceremony performed; but mamma has Argus backed through the ropes in the first round when it comes to watchfulness. If I could only find some way to separate Gwen from mamma for about an hour it would all be over but the shouting."

M. Kargovitch smiled pleasantly at his American friend.

"Let's have another of those delicious 'bronx' inspirations," he suggested; "it may inspire a solution of your problem."

When the waiter had brought the two drinks and set them upon the table, M. Kargovitch raised his glass to the American.

"My regards, my friend," he said. "I have been thinking, and I believe that I have found a way—listen;" and leaning across the table he bent close to Hemmington Main's ear, into which he whispered a heaven born plan.

When he had done Hemmington Main leaned back in his chair and laughed.

"I would never take you for that sort," he said; "and I don't give two whoops in hades if you are. You're right, Kargovitch—you're a right one; I'd trust you with my life, and my pocket book too; but I can promise you, on the credit and the word of Abner J. Bass that you'll be well paid if you can pull this thing off as you have outlined it. You won't have to depend on what we've got in our pockets—just name your price and it'll be paid."

"I promise you," said M. Kargovitch, "that my charge shall not be exorbitant. I have taken a fancy to you and your bronxes, and it may be that I shall not ask a kopek of reward. Promise me that you will let me name my own price when the thing is done, and accept the word of a gentleman that no advantage will be taken of you or your friends."

"Done!" cried Hemmington Main; and he extended his hand across the little round table to the tall young man who faced him.

"Now go," said Kargovitch, "and learn if you can when Argus and Io leave Demia, and the road that they will take."

CHAPTER SIX

WHEN Prince Boris of Karlova stepped from his limousine before the palace of Alexis III of Margoth, Ivan Kantchi was close at his elbow.

"Turn your helmet around," he whispered into the royal ear, "and keep it on. In the name of Heaven, don't take it off and wave it again. When you're saluted, return the salute."

"Shut up," growled the crown prince, "and don't forget that I'm a highness. You ought to have your head chopped off. When we get back to Karlova I'll see to it; but, Kantchi, my friend, if ever I do get back you'll never make a prince of me again—I'd rather hang to the nearest gibbet."

"Which would suit your highness's peculiar style of beauty far better than the purple," replied Ivan.

"Purple?" asked the crown prince. "I don't see no purple in this uniform. It's black and yellow."

"Hst!" warned Ivan; "Prince Stroebel is awaiting

your highness. Trip along with him, and when you're presented to the king don't act like a swineherd—remember that you're a prince."

The pseudo Prince Boris turned quickly to follow the instructions of his mentor. He took two or three rapid strides in the direction of the prime minister of Margoth, forgetful, for the instant, of the unaccustomed sabre which dangled at his side. The perverse weapon swung between his long legs, he tripped, stumbled, and lunged headlong upon the bemedalled breast of Prince Stroebel. His helmet tumbled from his head and rolled along the marble pavement; and one of his huge hands, grasping wildly for support jammed the helmet of the prime minister over that dignified official's ears, extinguishing him, momentarily.

From an upper window of the palace a pair of girlish eyes looked down upon the scene. A girlish giggle broke from a pair of red lips, and Princess Mary of Margoth threw herself upon the window seat and shook with laughter.

"Oh, Carlotta!" she cried. "Did you see him? And poor old Stroebel! It serves him right. It is he who is at the bottom of this ridiculous scheme to marry me to that hideous and impossible boor. He is even worse than I had imagined—from here I could see his red nose and his little, close-set eyes; but, Carlotta, we must hasten—the moment of the ordeal approaches. Oh, but won't Da-da be mad!"

"Yes, your highness, I think that he will," agreed Carlotta, with an unmistakable shudder.

"Come!" cried the Princess Mary, and seizing Carlotta by the hand she dragged that unhappy lady toward the door to the royal dressing room where, behind bar and bolt, the two worked assiduously with pencil and paste, and comb and brush for the better part of an hour.

The meeting between Alexis III of Margoth, and Crown Prince Boris of Karlova had passed off without any untoward incidents to greatly mar the felicity of the occasion. It is true that the royal Karlovian had seemed often at a loss as to just where to dispose his hands or feet to the best advantage; and that for a while he had sat with one long leg thrown in careless disorder over the arm of the great throne chair in which he sat beside his illustrious father-in-law-to-be, but on the whole he had gotten through the ordeal with much greater credit than he had won upon the streets of the capitol.

The great functionaries of the state, the little functionaries, the nobles, the ambassadors from foreign courts, and the high officers of the Margothian army had been presented to the royal visitor. The absence of Baron Kantchi, the Karlovian minister, was duly explained by the Karlovian military chargé d'affaires —Baron Kantchi had received only that morning an urgent command from his royal master to present himself at court in Sovgrad without delay. The chargé d'affaires looked rather frightened, uncomfortable and scandalized; but Ivan Kantchi, Alexander Palensk, and Nicholas Gregovitch supported him with such frightful glares that he managed to look almost happy as he kissed the large, red hand of Prince Boris of Karlova—happier by far than the prince.

At last the great doors at the far end of the throne room opened wide, the heavy hangings were drawn back. A court functionary in knee breeches and gold braid appeared in the opening.

"Her Royal Highness, Princess Mary Constantia Deodora Theresa Eugénie Sylvia!" he announced in reverent tones.

An aisle was opened from the doorway to the foot of the throne up on which a third chair had been placed for the princess. Every eye turned in the direction of the little figure walking slowly at the head of her ladies-in-waiting, and more than one Margothian smothered an exclamation of incredulity or horror as they saw the face of their beloved princess.

Prince Boris of Karlova, prodded by Ivan Kantchi, rose as the Princess Mary entered the room, and, with the other Karlovians who had not before seen the Margothian princess, strained his eyes in her direction. Trained in the etiquette of courts, the audience gave no token of the true emotions which surged beneath their resplendent costumes, as Mary of Margoth approached the throne to meet her future husband.

The Karlovians saw a small woman, bent, and supporting herself with a cane. The yellow skin of the forehead was lined with wrinkles. Dark rings circled the squinting eyes. The lower lip drooped, the upper was slightly raised, giving an expression of partial idiocy to the countenance, and exposing a dark spot where a front tooth was missing. The low cut bodice revealed a yellow, scrawny neck, creased with many lines.

Ivan Kantchi gave a mental gasp; but to all outward appearances he might have been looking for the first time upon the most beautiful woman in the world. Not so Prince Boris, however. His eyebrows went up, and he raised his palm to cover the grin which he made no effort to suppress.

"Name of a name!" he whispered to Ivan; "What a fright."

"Shut up, you fool!" snapped Kantchi. "She is a princess and a woman."

Alexis III rose to greet his daughter. A terrific frown darkened his brow; but he had seen the contemptuous smile upon the face of his royal guest, and anger and pride smothered the rebuke which he had been upon the point of delivering to his temerous daughter.

True to his coaching, The Rider raised the hand of Princess Mary to his lips. Like a parrot he repeated the words which Ivan Kantchi had taught him; but the only reply was a vacant stare from the squinting eyes of the princess, and a still further droop of the lower jaw. It was evident to the Karlovians present thet the Margothian princess was a hopeless idiot.

At last the painful audience was terminated. The king, Princess Mary, Prince Boris, Stroebel and Kantchi withdrew. The assemblage separated into little knots of animated gossipers, and with the restraint of royalty removed long restrained laughter attested the appreciation with which the Margothians had viewed the daring ruse which their clever little princess had adopted to discourage the matrimonial advances of the crown prince of Karlova.

As the king and Princess Mary passed out of the throne room together the former spoke in low tones to his daughter. His face was very white and stern; the arm upon which the little hand of Princess Mary rested, trembled to the anger which filled Alexis III.

"You have accomplished nothing," he said, "other than to make yourself and your king ridiculous in the eyes of our subjects and of strangers and to finally crystalize my determination that you shall wed Prince Boris. After seeing him I might have hesitated; but if he is a boor, what shall the king of Margoth say for his own daughter? It will be an excellent match, and I promise your highness that the betrothal shall take place upon the morrow."

In accordance with the program which the king and Prince Stroebel had arranged, Princess Mary and Prince Boris were to be given a half hour together alone, that they might become better acquainted, and pursuant to this idea the king, Stroebel, and Kantchi left them.

No sooner were the two alone than the princess rose, and hobbled slowly across the floor, leaning upon her cane. Without a word of apology or adieu she passed through a small doorway, and was gone. The door opened into a corridor near the foot of a staircase, and as the portal closed behind her Princess Mary straightened up, the stupid squint in her eyes was replaced by a mischievous twinkle, and a merry smile transformed the sagging jaw into a well moulded, aggressive little chin.

Gathering her royal robes half way to her knees, Princess Mary scampered up the stairway and along a wide hallway toward her own apartments. At a turning she came unexpectedly upon an officer on guard. Instantly the skirts dropped demurely about the trim ankles, the reckless gait became a dignified walk, though the roguish dimples still hovered about the corners of the piquant little mouth, and laughing eyes looked sideways at the stony-faced lieutenant standing rigidly at salute.

Once inside her own suite, the princess ran quickly toward the frightened and nervous Carlotta who advanced to meet her, her arms outstretched, and a question on her lips.

"Oh," cried the princess, "he is awful—just simply awful; and Da-da is so mad at me he could eat me alive. And, Carlotta, I'm going to run away!"

"Your highness!" almost screamed the scandalized Carlotta.

"But I am. Da-da was so angry that he swore that I should be betrothed to that frightful Karlovian person to-morrow, and I simply must get out of his clutches until he has had time to cool off."

"Oh, your highness, it is awful!" moaned Carlotta. "I knew what would come of an American education. Never before has a Margothian princess thought to question the commands of her father, the king. It is all due to those frightful, democratic ideas which you picked up in the New World."

As she talked, the faithful Carlotta was busy removing the state robes of her mistress while the latter grimaced at herself in an adjacent mirror that she might enjoy the ecstacy of contemplating the missing tooth and the network of wrinkles before Carlotta removed the last vestige of them to leave the fair, young face as clear and blemishless as marble and the firm, white teeth glistening in an unbroken row. In half an hour Mary was herself again. Her aggressive spirit had swept away the weak remonstrances of Carlotta to the bold plan the girl had conceived, and now there remained but to discuss the details and make the final arrangements.

As the two talked there came a knock upon the door and in reply to Carlotta's summons the king's secretary entered the chamber, halting inside the doorway and bowing very low. With a smile and a pleasant word the princess bid him advance. As she noted the man's hesitancy and embarrassment she broke into a merry laugh.

"I can guess your errand," she exclaimed. "You bear word of my punishment from His Majesty—I am to be shot at sunrise."

The secretary, who was a young man, blushed and smiled sheepishly. Then he cleared his throat once or twice.

"Not quite so bad as that, Your Highness," he replied. "His Majesty commands that you remain in your apartments until he summons you tomorrow. I am to return with your assurance that the king's command will be respected."

"And if I will not promise?" she asked, with one of her sweetest smiles.

"Then His Majesty directs that you be placed under arrest and a guard posted in the corridor before your apartments," replied the secretary.

"You are to return at once to His Majesty, I presume, with my assurances?" she asked.

"His Majesty has already departed for Klovia, where he dines this evening," replied the secretary. "I am merely to act for him, Your Highness. If you give me your promise to respect the king's wishes I am to receive them for His Majesty—if you do not, then I am to arrange for the guard."

"I see," said Princess Mary, and she rose and walked to and fro as though in deep thought. At last she paused before a small door in that part of the room opposite from the doorway through which the secretary had entered.

"I should like to have a few minutes in which to think the matter over, and talk with Carlotta," she said in a voice so sweet and with a smile so winning that it would have been impossible to deny her had she been but a goose-girl instead of a princess; "so, if you will step into this ante-chamber, M. Klein," and she laid her hand upon the knob and partially opened the door, "Carlotta and I will discuss the matter."

Now what is there to do when a princess of the blood royal condescends to hold a door open for one but to pass through, backward, in as courtly a manner as possible? Nothing, of course; and so the king's secretary backed into the little room, the Princess Mary cast a sweet smile upon, and the door closed—with an ominous click that was not entirely lost upon the gallant M. Klein.

Then he turned and looked about him to discover that he was in a very small room with a single heavily grated window high in one wall above his head—a small window which let in air but none too much light. M. Klein scratched his head and let his eyes return to the closed door. He was half tempted to turn the knob; but no, to enter the presence of Her Highness until bid would be an unpardonable offense. So M. Klein waited, shifting his weight from one foot to another, the pleasure of the little princess whom all Margoth loved.

And in the mean time the princess, aided by Carlotta, slipped into a long, dark colored cloak. Carlotta, too, garbed herself in bonnet and wrap, and the two, carrying themselves more like criminals than members of a royal household, sneaked out into the corridor and made their surreptitious way down back stairways to the rear of the palace. The royal stables lay not so far away, night was falling, and undetected the two fugitives presently appeared before a surprised and bowing chauffeur.

"The open car, Stefan," instructed Princess Mary; The old one without the arms, and take me west on the Roman road—I'll tell you just where to go, later."

CHAPTER SEVEN

HEMMINGTON Main rushed into the room of his new friend, Kargovitch.

"They're leaving this evening," he cried. "They only stopped here because one of the maids is sick. Mrs. Bass wants to get on to Sovgrad as soon as possible. I got it all from their chauffeur. She's heard rumors of trouble between Margoth and Karlova, and she's afraid they may be detained here if they delay. They're leaving both maids—the well one to look after the sick one—who are to follow on by rail later. You can't miss 'em—touring car with a chauffeur and two women. One of the women is middle age with greyish hair, the other is young and—beautiful."

"Good, I'll get them," replied Kargovitch. "Now

you take the next train for Sovgrad—it leaves in about twenty minutes. As soon as you get there get a couple of horses and a priest, and ride to Peter's Inn, anyone can direct you. Give this note to Peter, and he will send a guide with you who will conduct you to where I'll wait for you with the future Mrs. Main —and ma-ma's full and unqualified consent."

"Gad!" exclaimed Main, "she'll never forgive me."

"Probably not; but now go, there's no time to waste if you want to catch that train."

When his friend had departed M. Kargovitch strolled down to the hotel office, paid his bill, and walked out into the streets of Demia. There he bought a late afternoon paper in which appeared a carefully censored account of the visit of Crown Prince Boris of Karlova to the court of Alexis III. The article closed with the statement that "it is understood that Prince Boris will return to Sovgrad tonight following the banquet which the king is giving in his honor at the summer palace at Klovia."

There was no reference to the Princess Mary, or to the alliance between the two royal houses. In another column a few lines were devoted to the arrival of the wife and daughter of the famous American multi-millionaire, Abner J. Bass. M. Kargovitch was not the only person to read this latter item with interest. Princess Mary of Margoth saw it, and gave a little exclamation of surprise and delight, for she had known Gwendolyn Bass well at the select American boarding school to which the little princess had been sent at the instigation of Stroebel. The royal guest of

Alexis III saw it, and licked his lips sorrowfully at the thought that he was a prince and not a bandit—what a rich haul would be the wife and daughter of an American millionaire!

"Stefan," called Princess Mary as the machine rolled from the palace grounds, "the Hotel Royal first."

Carlotta asked questions and interposed objections, saying that they surely would be recognized; but Mary, accustomed to having her own way, overruled them all.

"I want to see Gwendolyn Bass," she announced. "She knows me only as Mary Banatoff, so she couldn't expose me even if she would. When I enter the hotel I'll draw my veil. It'll be safe enough."

When the car drew up before the hotel the two alighted and entered. At the office they obtained the number of the Bass suite, and saying that they were old friends, took the elevator and ascended without being announced.

A maid admitted them, and as Princess Mary stepped into the room and threw back her veil Gwendolyn Bass gave a little cry of astonished pleasure as she ran forward to greet her friend.

For half an hour the two girls chattered on as fast as their tongues would go. Mary Banatoff was "so sorry that you are not going to be in Demia longer, and next time be sure to let me know; and Mrs. Bass you must be very brave to travel the Roman road into Sovgrad at night, with The Rider abroad. He is a frightful wretch. Have your chauffeur drive at top speed after you pass the border."

While they talked Stefan sat rigidly in the driver's seat of the waiting car. A horseman rode up from behind and at sight of the car drew rein. Then he approached close to Stefan's side.

"Whose car is this?" he asked.

Stefan looked up to see a tall military figure bending toward him. The man was not in uniform and Stefan did not recognize him; but Stefan had a guilty conscience because he knew that the excursion of his young mistress was entirely irregular. He hesitated.

"I asked," said the stranger, "whose car this is. Does it belong to the Americans by the name of Bass who are travelling to Sovgrad tonight?"

Stefan grasped at the suggested straw.

"Yes, monsieur," he replied, "it is the Bass car."

"And are you leaving at once?"

"Yes, monsieur." Stefan could have strangled the man for his impudence. The very idea of questioning him, Stefan, the royal chauffeur, in this familiar manner!

"Good," said the stranger, and rode on leaving Stefan sputtering ragefully.

Slowly he turned the next corner, and when out of sight of Stefan spurred his horse into a trot. At the end of the city street, where it broke into the open country and the Roman road, the trot was quickened to a gallop.

"I'll never make it," muttered the rider. "What the devil are they leaving so early for? Well, I suppose

©Lorillard 1974

KENT

Micronite filter.
Mild, smooth taste.
America's quality cigarette.
Kent.

ng Size or
eluxe 100's.

Try the crisp, clean taste of Kent Menthol.

The only Menthol with the famous Micronite filter.

one place is as good as another; but I should have preferred Karlovian territory—it might raise the devil should I happen to be caught in Margoth."

At about the same time Mary Banatoff bade farewell to her American friend and descended with the faithful Carlotta to the waiting car.

"Drive slowly, Stefan," she said, "for the night is beautiful. I am going to Vitza."

"Yes, Your Highness," replied Stefan.

"S-s-sh!" cautioned the princess, "someone might hear you."

"Yes, Your Highness," said Stefan.

Princess Mary sank back into the cushions of the tonneau with a smile and a sigh of resignation.

"The safest thing, Carlotta," she said, "is not to speak to Stefan at all."

The road to Vitza leaves the Roman road about ten miles west of Demia, and runs north through the mountains for another ten miles to the favorite palace of the king of Margoth. Stefan drove slowly as he had been instructed. The moon shown brilliantly down from a cloudless sky, and Princess Mary was enjoying to the full every moment of her adventure. She would remain in Vitza for a few days until the king's anger had blown over, as it always did blow over when the Princess Mary transgressed. Then she would come back and forgive her father, and everything would be as it had been before. Da-da would never force her to marry that frightful, hideous Prince Boris!

As the car turned north into the hills, and wound

slowly back and forth up the steep grade just before leaving the Roman road to enter the road to Vitza a horseman drew rein at the summit of a particularly steep and tortuous stretch, and turning looked back into the valley beneath and behind him.

The lights of a car shown for a moment far in his rear, and then were lost in a sudden turning of the road. The man drew a black mask from his pocket and adjusted it over the lower part of his face. Then he reined his mount close behind a shoulder of rock at a sharp turning of the road, where the shadows veiled him from the sight of the approaching way-farers. The fingers of his right hand gripped the butt of a long and formidable looking revolver, while those of his left curbed the nervous sidesteppings of his restive mount.

Slowly the big car wound its way up the steep grade. The gears, meshed in second speed, protested loudly, while the exhaust barked in sympathy through an open muffler. Stefan, outwardly calm, was inwardly boiling, as was the water in the radiator before him threatening to do. Silent, but none the less sincere, were the curses where with he cursed the fate which had compelled him to drive "the old car" up Vitza grade which the new car took in high with only a gentle purring.

Almost at the summit there is a curve about a projecting shoulder of rock, and at this point the grade is steepest. More and more slowly the old car moved when it reached this point—there came from the steel and aluminum lungs a few consumptive coughs which racked the car from bumper to tail light, and as Stefan shifted quickly from second to low the wheels almost stopped, and at the same instant a horseman reined quickly into the center of the road before them, a levelled revolver pointing straight through the frail windshield at the unprotected breast of the astonished Stefan.

"Stand and deliver!" cried a menacing voice that sent a delightful little shiver through the frame of Her Royal Highness, the Princess Mary.

The horseman was directly in front of the car. Stefan was both quick witted and courageous. One single burst of speed and both horse and man would be ridden down. The gears were in low, the car was just at a standstill. Stefan pressed his foot upon the accelerator and let in the clutch. The car should have jumped forward and crushed the life from the presumptuous bandit; but it did nothing of the sort. Instead, it gave voice to a pitiful choking sound, and died.

"Get out!" commanded the brigand.

Stefan set the emergency brake and climbed down into the road. He had played his last trick—there was nothing left to do but obey. Princess Mary was beside him almost as soon as he touched the ground.

"Don't let him know who we are," she warned in a low whisper.

Carlotta followed her mistress, and as she took her place beside her she clasped the latter's hand in hers. The robber dismounted and approached them, and for a moment examined his captives intently.

"One is young and beautiful," was his mental comment; "the other of middle age, with greyish hair," and then, aloud: "Mrs. Bass, you and your daughter will kindly re-enter the machine."

Princess Mary gasped, and squeezed Carlotta's hand. He took them for the Americans! Princess Mary could have danced, so elated was she. So long as the bandit was ignorant of her true identity the chances of trapping him were greatly enhanced; and, too, while the ransom for a rich American's daughter might be large, that which he would demand for a princess of the royal blood would be infinitely greater.

She wondered if this could really be the notorious Rider, this quiet-voiced man, who held open the car door for her and assisted Carlotta and herself back into the tonneau. She had always pictured The Rider as a low and brutal type of man, ignorant, unlettered, boorish; but this bandit had spoken to them in the purest of English. Could it be that The Rider was an American or an Englishman. If so he would speak the common language of Karlova and Margoth in the low vernacular of the underworld, if he spoke it all. She would try him.

"To whom," she asked in her own tongue, "are we indebted for this little surprise? Can it be that we have been honored by the famous Rider?"

The man laughed.

"You have been honored more than you can know, mademoiselle," he replied. "Yes I am The Rider; but you need have no fear if you do as I ask—I only kill those who disobey me,"—the last in a very fierce and terrible voice.

Princess Mary felt a tremor of nervous excitement —a delicious little thrill—run up and down her royal spine. Ah, here was Romance! Here was Adventure! She wished that he would remove his mask—she would like to see the features of this redoubtable brigand who was the terror of two kingdoms—the scourge of the border. Doubtless, she thought, the revealment would prove most unpoetic—a pock marked face, brutal features, the lines which Crime and Vice stamp indelibly upon the countenances of their votaries. On second thought, she preferred that he remain masked, for even though he had answered her in as good Margothian as her own she could not believe that so low a fellow could fail to reflect in his personal appearance his degraded associations and environment.

And now The Rider turned to Stefan. "My man," he said, "we are about to effect an exchange. For the honor of driving your mistress and her daughter I shall relinquish to you my faithful steed. Be careful of him—he possesses a pedigree which fills four large volumes and runs back to the royal stud which The Great King presented to the emperor Diocletian after the victories of Galerius in Persia. When you are through with him return him to the royal stables of the King of Karlova, from which he was stolen. Mount, Stefan, and ride back to Demia."

The royal chauffeur hesitated. The Rider raised his

revolver until the dark hole of the muzzle was on a line with Stefan's diaphragm.

"Hasten, Stefan," he admonished, and Stefan hastened.

The Rider watched the chauffeur until the latter had covered several hundred yards of the road toward Demia; then he climbed into the driver's seat and started the car once more upon its interrupted journey.

As they passed the road leading to Vitza, and the princess realized that their captor was keeping to the Roman road in the direction of the border the gravity of her predicament was borne in upon her. At first she had viewed the affair as one might view a pleasurable adventure which broke the dull monotony of existence; but as the minutes passed and gave her opportunity for reflection she saw all too plainly the grave dangers of her position. Her one thought now was of escape; and the wild nature of the country through which the road passed, together with the many steep ascents which often brought the car almost to a dead stop, offered her every hope of success.

And so it was that near the summit of a particularly bad grade, while the chugging of the exhaust and the grinding of the gears obliterated all lesser sounds, the two doors of the tonneau opened simultaneously. The Princess Mary leaped lightly out upon the right and Carlotta essayed the same feat upon the left. All would have gone well and their escape, doubtless, been assured had Carlotta been favored by the advantages of an American education, which teaches one many things that may be found in no text book or in the curriculum of any college.

But Carlotta's education had been sadly neglected, in some respects at least, which may account for the fact that she stepped from the slowly moving car with her face to the rear. The result was only what might have been expected; and Carlotta, to avoid the wheels, rolled quickly to one side and just far enough to come within the range of the tail of the bandit's left eye. It was just a glimpse he got of something moving in the road behind him; but it was enough to bring his head around and reveal to his view the scrambling figure of Carlotta as she staggered to her feet and bolted down the hill in the direction from which they had just come.

Another glance showed the brigand that the tonneau was empty. The car stopped with a jerk, and almost in the same instant The Rider was in the road, his revolver in his hand, and his quick eyes piercing the night for a sign of his escaped prisoners.

The Princess Mary, crouching close to the rocky side of the cut through which the road passed at this point, saw the car stop, and guessing that their escape had been discovered, turned and ran after the fleeing Carlotta.

She had covered but a few yards when there came from behind her a sharp, peremptory command to halt. The Princess Mary, unaccustomed to obeying commands of any nature, ignored this one. It was repeated once, immediately followed by the report of a shot. The Princess Mary came to a dead stop, and turned upon her pursuer. Her little chin was high in the air, her eyes flashed; but her lower lip trembled just a trifle as she faced the man who now came running up.

"How dare you!" she cried. "How dare you fire upon—" and then she hesitated. For the moment she had forgotten that she was only Miss Bass of America.

Carlotta, turning at the sound of the shot, came quickly back to the side of her mistress. The bandit looked at the two, and even in the darkness Princess Mary thought that she detected the shadow of a smile beneath his black mask.

"I am very sorry, Miss Bass," he said; "but really you mustn't try that again—it's awfully dangerous, leaping from a moving car. Permit me," and he offered his arm to escort her back to the machine.

The girl ignored the little gallantry, and very stiffly and haughtily walked back up the hill, while the bandit followed at her elbow. He made her take the seat beside him this time, while Carlotta resumed her place in the tonneau.

"It will be safer thus," he explained. "I should hate to have you risk your life again in an attempt to escape, and I can watch you better here. You'll have to act as hostage, you know. I'm sure your mother won't try to get away again as long as I have you safely beside me. Hadn't you better put this robe around your shoulders? the night air is a trifle chill," and he turned and attempted to place the robe for her.

"I do not wish a robe," snapped the Princess Mary. "You will kindly confine yourself to your proper role —that of brigand and captor. You will get your ransom money, and in the mean time you will oblige me by not speaking to me—I have no desire to converse with a thief and a murderer."

"You mustn't be too hard on me, Miss Bass," expostulated The Rider; "I haven't killed anyone for a week, really. You can't imagine how hard times have been, and the last one not only bled all over me but when I came to empty his pockets I found that he didn't possess the price of a bottle of good wine. You have no idea, Miss Bass, how discouraging this business is at times."

Princess Mary shuddered. The fellow was a hopeless brute. Carlotta, in the tonneau, trembled. What, O what would the man not do to them when he discovered that they were not the wife and daughter of the rich American? He would never get a royal princess off his hands without jeopardizing his head, and Carlotta was convinced that he would murder them both and bury their bodies in some mountain ravine to hide the evidences of his guilt when he should discover the terrible mistake he had made.

The Rider, after several ineffectual attempts to draw Miss Bass into conversation, desisted; and in silence the little party sped onward toward the mountains which form the natural boundary between Margoth and Karlova.

At a point just beyond the frontier, the bandit turned the car into a narrow wagon road, where it was hidden from the main highway by a screen of trees and undergrowth. The road upon which it stood was little more than an opening among the trees. Once it had been used as a wood road, but since the king of Karlova had forbidden the further cutting of timber in this district it had been unused by others than The Rider and his disreputable following.

A few yards from the Roman road the car was brought to a stop. The bandit extinguished the lights and turning to the captive at his side announced that they would be compelled to complete their journey on foot, as no machine could travel the rough and precipitous trail ahead of them.

"You expect me to walk?" she asked, icily.

"Unless you prefer to be carried," he replied.

"I shall neither walk nor be carried," she announced.

"Yonder," said The Rider, pointing through the darkness amidst the surrounding trees, "is a little mound of earth. Beneath it lies a misguided lady who refused to walk. Unfortunately she was too heavy to carry. I can carry you; but in the mean time your mother might escape and lead the gendarmes to my hiding place; so, if you refuse to come with me, I shall be compelled to kill your mother and carry you."

Carlotta felt the cold shivers run up and down her spine. Princess Mary turned upon The Rider.

"You beast!" she exclaimed.

"You will walk then?" he asked, suavely.

Upward through the impenetrable blackness the three stumbled. Even The Rider seemed to know the path none too well, and the Princess could not but wonder at his obvious ignorance of the way. Often he stopped and examined the ground beneath the rays of a small pocket flash-lamp, and twice they were compelled to retrace their steps when it became evident that they had lost the trail.

Romance and Adventure were commencing to pall upon the Princess Mary. Her back ached and her legs were like two heavy logs of wood.

CHAPTER EIGHT

WHEN, earlier in the day, Prince Boris of Karlova had been released for a few hours from the appalling ceremonies of royal hospitality, and was alone in his apartments with the faithful Ivan, Nicholas, and Alexander he had begged of them to save him from a repetition of the frightful experiences of the morning.

"I'd rather go to the gibbet," he growled.

"Which you would doubtless grace to advantage," replied Ivan. "Each of us has his appointed place in the universal scheme of things—yours is not the throne."

The prince scowled, and then, after a moment's silence: "At least I make as good a prince as that hideous little half-wit does a princess."

"Granted," exclaimed Ivan with a grimace. "If

Boris could but see what was destined for him! Thank the Lord he was spared the ordeal, for he is such a good natured fellow that he might have acquiesced out of pity for her and brought a toothless idiot to the throne of Karlova. As it is our little substitution may save Karlova from a war with Margoth, since there is little likelihood that his majesty, Alexis III, will be over keen to have you for a son-in-law, and so will view with relief your indifference to his royal daughter. If Boris himself had come things would have been different. Alexis could not have but looked with favor upon him, and his refusal to marry the Princess Mary would have resulted in precipitating the long-brewing war—not, however, that we would not welcome a war with these contemptible Margothians."

"I am not interested in history," growled the crown prince. "At present I am interested in but one thing, and that is to get as far away from that frightful state dinner at Klovia as possible."

"You wished to be a prince, my friend," Nicholas reminded him, "and state dinners are a part of the penalty of being a prince."

"I have had all of this prince business that I care for," replied the other, scowling. "Get me out of here. Get me back to Peter's Inn, and let me go my way. I am sick of seeing people laugh at me behind their hands, and even openly as they did in the streets this morning. If you do not get me out of here I will reveal the truth to the king of Margoth before I am an hour older."

The three noble conspirators saw that the man was in earnest. They were far from loath to humor him, since they themselves had felt the sting and the burden of embarrassment since they had entered Margoth in his company.

It was Alexander Palensk who first suggested a feasible plan of escape from the impossible position in which the levity of the true Boris had placed them all. It was, in short, to wait until dark, and then hurry away on the Roman road for Sovgrad, after sending word to Alexis at Klovia that Prince Boris had been taken suddenly ill with what appeared to be a mild attack of ptomaine poisoning. Ivan Kantchi was to bear the message and apologies.

And thus it was that the pseudo prince and his two companions rode out of Demia under the cover of darkness that very evening while Ivan Kantchi made his way to Klovia with the excuses of his royal master to the king of Margoth.

It was evident to the young noble that Alexis was far from displeased to be rid of his gauche guest, and as a result Ivan could not resist the temptation to bait the Margothian ruler.

"It is evident, Sire," he said, "that the charms of her royal highness, Princess Mary, have captivated my prince; and I trust that I may be the bearer of the glad tidings to him that his suit is looked upon with favor by both your majesty and her royal highness."

For a moment Alexis III was silent. It was apparent that he labored under the stress of powerful emotions which he would have gladly hidden; but at last indignation got the better of diplomacy and he blurted out his true feelings to the friend and confidante of the Karlovian prince.

"My god, sir," he cried, "do you think for a moment that I would give the hand of my daughter to the ill-bred boor who disgraced my capitol today, to the monkey who was the laughing stock of all Demia?"

Ivan Kantchi forgot for the moment the truth of the other's statements. He thought only of the affront that had been put upon the name of his friend and prince. His face went white, and he straightened very stiffly as he replied in a cold, ironic tone.

"By leaving thus under the cloak of simulated illness Prince Boris but endeavored to spare you the knowledge of his true sentiments—sentiments which were shared by all those Karlovians who looked upon the Princess Mary to-day. Do I make myself quite plain, Your Majesty?"

Alexis III flushed, rose from his chair, and without another word turned his back upon the ambassador of the Karlovian prince and left the apartment.

Ivan shrugged and turned away toward the door that had opened to admit him to the presence. As he passed out of the palace his lips formed a sentence in which at least one word was repeated several times —a word which sounded much like 'war.'

CHAPTER NINE

For a matter of half an hour M. Klein awaited the pleasure of the little Princess Mary of Margoth; but receiving no summons and hearing no sound from the chamber beyond he at last ventured to knock upon the door of the tiny room into which the princess had herself ushered him. There was no response to his knocking, which he repeated at intervals for several minutes. Then he called aloud the name of his princess, to be answered only by silence. M. Klein became more and more perturbed in spirit. He still hesitated to turn the knob and enter the apartment of her royal highness without first obtaining permission, but at last he grew desperate. The knob turned beneath his fingers, he pressed outward with increasing vigor, but the door did not open—M. Klein was a prisoner. It came to him with the sudden shock of an unexpected douche of cold water; and it made him tremble all over and gasp, too, as the water might have.

For a moment or two he stood looking dumbly at the blank panels of the door. Knowing the Princess Mary as he did he was quite positive that his imprisonment was not a matter of chance; but what would the king say! At the thought M. Klein went white, and commenced to beat violently upon the door, shouting in the mean while at the top of his voice. There was no response.

The afternoon waned, and darkness came. M. Klein was exhausted by his vain efforts at attracting attention. The little, grated window had proved too high for him to reach, and had only served to admonish him of the flight of time as the afternoon light which it shed within his tiny prison waned and faded into the blackness of night.

The secretary became frantic. His calls for help rose finally to wild shrieks. He pounded upon the door. He kicked it, and continually he cursed himself for a silly ass in thus permitting a slip of a girl to put him in so ridiculous and dangerous a position. The king would never forgive him—he would be lucky if Alexis did not throw him into prison.

For the twentieth time he leaped for the grating of the window above him. His fingers caught and held. He drew himself up until his face was at the opening, and then he opened his mouth and gave vent to a piercing scream for help.

Below in the courtyard a sentry pacing to and fro heard the wild cry. Instantly his own voice rose in a sharp summons for the non-commissioned officer of the guard. The scream from above was repeated as a sergeant came upon a run from the guard house.

"Who calls?" cried the sentry.

M. Klein's fingers were relaxing their hold upon the grating. He had only time to cry: "Princess Mary's apartments!" before they slipped and let him drop back to the floor of his prison.

But the sergeant had heard, and so had the sentry; and a moment later an officer of the guard followed by a score of armed men were dashing through the corridors of the palace, up stairs, and along passage-ways until they came to the suite of the Princess Mary.

And here they permitted no courtly etiquette to detain them, but throwing open the doors bolted into the forbidden precincts of the royal apartments. A moment later M. Klein was released and, bundled into an automobile, was speeding toward Klovia, his heart in his mouth and his brain a-whirl with the stupendous fact that the Princess Mary had fled the royal palace.

At about the same time Stefan, mounted upon the abandoned horse of the highwayman, was spurring along the Roman road into Demia. Through the streets of the ancient capitol he raced, regardless of gendarmes and speed laws, upon his way to Klovia and his king.

Alexis III, relieved of the embarrassment of his

royal guest, was giving himself over to the pleasures of the society of his own nobility, when a very much excited and dishevelled young man dashed unannounced into the banquet hall, throwing aside and upsetting a couple of guardsmen who had thought to interrupt his impetuous progress. To the king's side the young man made his way, while the guardsmen, picking themselves from the floor, pursued him.

"Klein!" exclaimed the king. "What is the meaning of this?"

"O, pardon, Sire!" cried the excited secretary, falling upon his knees. "It is awful!"

"What is awful?" demanded the king, rising.

The guests too rose from their seats. The guardsmen, seeing now who their quarry was, halted beside the kneeling Klein. The king extended his hand and lifted the trembling secretary to his feet.

"Quick, man!" he cried. "What brings you here? What has happened?"

"The Princess Mary!" sobbed the overwrought secretary. "She has run away. She locked me in a closet, and then she ran away."

A poorly suppressed titter ran around the banquet board. Even the king smiled.

"I cannot say that I blame her, Klein," he said, "can you?"

The secretary rose, dumbfounded. He had expected the wrath of his sovereign to be poured upon his head, and instead he found anything but anger in the aspect and the tones of the king.

"She would have been no Margothian princess had

she willingly consented to mate with that Karlovian swineherd," said Prince Stroebel, who sat at the king's right. "Even I would rather have war with Constans of Karlova than see our beloved princess wed to the impossible boor whom we had among us this morning."

"I am glad that you have come to your senses, Stroebel," said the king, and then, turning to his secretary; "Come, Klein, don't look so downhearted. We forgive you. Her Highness has doubtless, gone to Vitza—she always goes to Vitza when she is angry with me. Inform Captain Polnik that it is our wish that he ride at once to Vitza and see that her highness has arrived safely."

The king was still speaking when an officer of the guard entered the room hastily and approached the ruler.

"And now what, Polnik?" asked Alexis, looking up at the white face and startled eyes of the officer.

"My God, your majesty," blurted the guardsman, "it is awful. Stefan has just ridden in with the most frightful news of the Princess Mary——"

Alexis leaped to his feet. His face went as white as that of the soldier before him.

"What has happened?" he cried in a hoarse voice. "Quick, man! Tell me," and then, his eyes chancing to glance in the direction of the doorway, he espied Stefan leaning, wide eyed, against the frame. "Here, Stefan!" he called. "Come here, man, and tell us your story."

Hatless, dust covered, and trembling, Stefan staggered across the room where he would have fallen to one knee before the king had not the latter deterred him with an impatient snap of his fingers.

"Your story, Stefan!" demanded Alexis. "What has happened to the Princess Mary?"

"The Rider, Sire," cried Stefan. "The Rider held us up upon the highway, and at the point of a pistol drove me away. Then he entered the machine and taking the wheel himself rôde off with her highness and Mademoiselle Carlotta. It happened just before we turned from the Roman road into the Vitza way. I mounted his horse, Sire, and rode here as fast as the beast could go. That is all, Sire!"

"God knows it is enough," cried Alexis. "Captain Polnik, turn out the guard. Impress into your service as many of the private machines as you may need, in addition to the military and royal cars at your disposal here, to transport your men in pursuit. Lose no time. At the border scatter your forces in both directions, unless you strike the trail before, and search the mountains thoroughly—The Rider lairs somewhere not far from the Roman road. We will go at once to Demia where you will keep us advised of the progress of your search. Do not cross into Karlova except under the most pressing necessity, though I do not need tell you that I shall expect you to cross even into Hell, if necessary, to rescue Her Highness from the clutches of that Devil's spawn."

"No, Sire," replied Polnik, "we of The Guard need not be told that."

"Good! Now go. In the meantime we will wire

Sovgrad to co-operate with us from their side of the border."

Captain Polnik saluted and left the hall. The guests who had risen when the king rose, were now talking excitedly among themselves. Those who were officers of The Guard were hastening from the palace to join their men. All was bustle and excitement. The courtly form and ceremony of a royal function were forgotten or ignored. In the mind of each Margothian there but a single thought loomed, large and ominous—their beloved princess was in the hands of that notorious cutthroat and scoundrel, The Rider. In fifteen minutes from the time that Captain Polnik left the banquet hall twenty automobiles carrying a hundred and fifty officers and soldiers of The Guard were racing toward the Roman road on their way to the western frontier.

CHAPTER TEN

SEVERAL miles ahead of them two other automobiles sped westward. In the foremost car rode Mrs. Abner J. Bass and her daughter, Gwendolyn—in the second the false Prince Boris with Alexander Palensk and Nicholas Gregovitch rode in moody silence, bound for the hunting lodge of the crown prince of Karlova, where The Rider and the prince were again to exchange identities and take up once more the particular roles for which each was best suited.

"I hope Boris will be there," said Alexander.

"Peter can get word to him quickly enough if he is not," replied the bandit. "If he is not there he will be in my camp—if the gendarmes haven't got him."

Nicholas laughed. "Gad!" he exclaimed, "what a joke on Boris, if they should."

"And on us, too," growled Alexander. "It would cost us our commissions should His Majesty ever learn our part in this affair. Say! what have we here?" as the car turned to one side and came to a stop beside another machine which blocked the road at a bad turn.

The royal chauffeur was excitedly berating the driver of the other car for stopping in such a place.

"Get out of there!" he cried. "Make way for His Royal Highness, Prince Boris of Karlova."

"Gwan, you Dago," growled the man addressed. "Talk American. Wotinel do you tink I AM?"

If her chauffeur had failed to understand the speech of the Karlovian, Mrs. Abner J. Bass had not. 'His Royal Highness, Prince Boris of Karlova!' Mrs. Bass was out in the dust of the Roman road in a second.

"McDougal!" she cried sharply. "Have a care! Prince Boris of Karlova is in that car."

"I don't givadam whose in dat car," grumbled the exasperated American who had been tinkering with a refractory magneto. "If he tinks I can pack a tourin' car off on me back he's got annuder tink comin'."

The three men had now descended from the royal limousine, the two officers having seen that a woman was in distress, and the bandit following their example from force of habit.

"I am so sorry, your highness," apologized Mrs. Bass, looking questioningly from one of the men to another; but none of them seemed desirous of acknowledging himself crown prince of Karlova. It was at this moment that Gwendolyn stepped from the car to her mother's side.

At sight of her face The Rider raised his military cap and bowed low.

"Permit me," he said, "to offer my services. I am Prince Boris of Karlova."

Mrs. Bass and her daughter curtsied. Alexander and Nicholas raised their helmets, bowing low from the hips.

"I am Mrs. Abner J. Bass of America," said the wife of the multi-millionaire, "and this is my daughter."

The Rider licked his lips. He had heard of the millions of the famous Abner J. Bass. What a haul!

"If you will permit me to offer you the use of my car," he said, "I will gladly take you to Sovgrad. My aides will remain with your chauffeur and see that he gets in safely after he has made the necessary repairs."

Alexander and Nicholas bit their lips and scowled. The affrontery of the man! Nicholas looked at Alexander. What were they to do? They had given their promises to respect the exchange which their prince had made with the highwayman, and to treat the latter as their lord and master until the true Boris claimed his rightful position. Alexander shrugged, and bowed in acquiescence. The Rider held open the door of the royal car, and assisted the two ladies to enter. Then he followed them.

"Good evening, my friends!" he called through the

window to the two officers as the car started once more upon its interrupted journey.

As the car bowled along the road The Rider thought rapidly. It never would do to enter Sovgrad in the royal car, nor could he hope to hold his precious prizes within the boundaries of the capitol city. Picking up the speaking tube he signalled the driver.

"To the hunting lodge," he said; "but stop first at Peter's Inn." And then to Mrs. Bass: "It is a long way to Sovgrad—we will stop for a moment at my hunting lodge for refreshments."

Mrs. Abner J. Bass, quite overcome by this close communion with royalty would have agreed to anything.

"How thoughtful of your highness," she murmured.

In the dim light The Rider could see that the younger of his victims was extremely beautiful. To her he addressed most of his remarks. He told her of the attempt to marry him to the Margothian princess, and during the narration an inspiration came to the unscrupulous scoundrel, which almost caused him to laugh aloud.

"You see," he said, "I must marry at once, someone whom I could love, or I shall be forced to marry this hideous woman. Of course if I marry another I cannot marry the princess."

"It would seem that it should be easy to find many desirable princesses who would be honored by such an alliance," suggested Mrs. Bass.

"But she need not be a princess," The Rider hastened to assure her. "In fact I should much prefer marrying one who is not a princess," and he looked directly and pointedly at Miss Gwendolyn Bass.

Mrs. Abner J. Bass gasped and almost choked. For once in her life she was at a loss as to what to say. A real Prince—a crown prince! and he had as much as said that he would like to marry Gwendolyn. 'Her Royal Highness, the Crown Princess Gwendolyn!' My! how wonderful it sounded! And later, Queen Gwendolyn! Mrs. Bass was thankful that she had chosen a really distinguished name for her daughter.

Miss Bass, who had seen quite all she desired to of the royal features, shrank far back into her corner of the car, a little shiver of horror playing up and down her spine. What had become of Hemmy? She was sure that she had caught a glimpse of him in Bucharest, and that her mother had seen him there, for immediately Mrs. Bass had altered her plans and turned back toward the west. She needed him now, if ever she had needed anyone, for she was not so blind but that she could read all too plainly the trend of the thoughts of the man at her side, and she knew her mother quite well enough to be sure that that ambitious lady would jump at the chance to become the mother-in-law of a prince of the blood-royal. But Hemmy might have been dead and buried, thought the girl, for all the good he could do her now. She hadn't the faintest idea as to where she might reach him.

The man at her side had been talking earnestly with her mother, now he had turned and was speaking to her. At first she only half comprehended the words which fell so easily from his lips and which, although she had been expecting them sooner or later, came now with all the effect of an unlooked for nervous shock.

"Your mother approves," he was saying, "and I hope, Miss Bass, that you will approve. It would be a very advantageous marriage." He neglected to specify to whose advantage it would redound. "The ceremony may be performed at my hunting lodge tonight—should we delay the king might get wind of the matter, and that would be the end of it, for I assure you that he would prevent our marriage and immediately place me under arrest."

"But I scarcely know you," objected the girl, "and anyway I do not wish to marry."

"Gwendolyn!" admonished Mrs. Bass. "His highness has honored you highly by asking your hand in marriage—of course you will accept him," and, turning to The Rider, "She is so young, and this has come to her so suddenly, you cannot wonder, your highness, that she is quite taken off her feet; but of course she will do as I say—Gwendolyn always does, she is a very good and dutiful daughter."

It was well for the peace of mind of Mrs. Abner J. Bass that she could not read what was at that moment passing through the mind of her dutiful daughter.

During the remainder of the ride the bandit regaled his mother-in-law-to-be with vivid word pictures of the wonders of his royal palaces, the power and glory of his house, and the riches of the domain over which he and the daughter of the house of Bass would one day rule.

Mrs. Bass became quite excited in anticipation; but Gwendolyn, inclined to captiousness in all that pertained to her royal fiancé, saw only the crudeness of his grammar, the coarseness of his voice, and the boorishness of his manners.

Presently the car turned from the Roman road into a dark wood, and shortly after drew up before a squalid inn. The Rider excused himself and entered the place on the pretext of arranging for a messenger to fetch a priest from a near-by monastery.

Inside he sought and found Peter to whom he transmitted his instructions. "I shall be at the royal hunting lodge," he said, "and when the priest comes here, have him brought there to me at once; but do not let him know where he is being taken. Lose no time about it either. If I have any other instructions for you I will send them in writing by a messenger," and with that he turned and hurried back to the waiting car.

CHAPTER ELEVEN

Now the road which leads north past Peter's Inn toward the Hunting lodge of the king of Karlova is not an automobile road. It passes beneath the heavy foliage of a dense forest, and as a result is seldom thoroughly dried out. Ox carts with broad tires travel it, carrying provisions to the lodge, and market stuff to Sovgrad from the few wretched little farms which eke out a miserable existence upon the borders of the hunting preserve. Royalty and its guests pass to and fro upon horse back; but automobiles seldom if ever hazard the soft mud and the deep ruts of what is doubtless one of the most abominable roads in Europe.

Rain had not fallen for many weeks, and as a result the road was reasonably hard, but the deep chuck holes retarded the speed of the car to such an extent that it travelled but little faster than a man might walk.

Peter had dispatched one of his dependents to fetch the priest The Rider had demanded, and was waiting for the man's return when the door of his barroom opened to admit two strangers. The first to enter was quite evidently a foreigner—a young man in riding togs and with a face which betokened a super-abundance of initiative and determination. At his heels followed a dark robed priest. Peter eyed the two questioningly.

"Good evening!" said the young man. "Have I the honor of addressing the proprietor of this charming hostelry?"

Peter nodded.

"Then your name is Peter?" asked the stranger.

Again Peter signified an affirmative, and the other drew a folded note from his pocket, extending it to the inn-keeper. "For you, my friend," he said.

Peter took the note, slowly unfolded it, and, with evident labor, spelled out the message it contained: "Peter:—Furnish the bearer with a guide who will conduct him and the priest to the spot where The Wolf lairs. Ask no questions. The Rider." That was all. Peter turned the paper over; but it was blank upon the opposite side. He looked from it to the young man and then on to the priest. How the devil had this young fellow come to be here so soon with a priest, and what had become of the messenger whom Peter had sent to fetch a priest? But the note said plainly that he must ask no questions. Peter scratched his head. The whole thing was a puzzle to him. Well, it was none of his business anyway, and here was a priest, and here was a written command from The Rider himself—there was naught to do but obey. He stepped close to the young man and whispered in his ear. The latter looked relieved, for Peter had just told him that his new friend had passed the Inn but a short time since and that he had come in an automobile which had remained in the darkness of the trees beside the road.

And so it happened that Hemmington Main and the priest he had brought from Sovgrad started off with their guide upon the road toward the royal hunting lodge before the automobile containing the false prince and his two victims had covered more than half the distance from the inn to their destination.

All during the journey Gwendolyn Bass' brain was a-whirl with mad schemes for escape from the fate which the ambitions of her mother had ordained for her; but nowhere, through the impenetrable darkness of the forest road, could she find an opportunity to put to the test of action a single one of them, and at last the machine turned into the royal preserves onto a fairly good road where the speed of the machine made escape without injury impossible.

The few servants at the hunting lodge had received their instructions from Prince Boris at the time when he had exchanged identities with The Rider, and now they welcomed the returning bandit as though he had indeed been the son of King Constans of Karlova, though once out of his presence their sneers of contempt were unrestrained.

At The Rider's command the two women were shown to apartments on the second floor, and while they removed the dust of the road from their garments and faces a lunch was served in a small breakfast room on the main floor of the lodge.

The three had scarcely seated themselves at the table before a servant appeared to announce the arrival of a young man accompanied by a priest.

"Ah!" exclaimed The Rider; "they arrived sooner than I had hoped. Show the good man in, and take care of his guide in the servants' quarters."

But when the priest was ushered into the breakfast room, his 'guide' followed close at his heels, though a servant in the royal livery did his best to prevent him. Gwendolyn Bass was the first to see the face of the young man behind the priest and at sight of it she half rose from her chair with a little exclamation of relief and surprise.

"Hemmy!" she cried, and at the name Mrs. Bass turned and saw Mr. Hemmington Main standing directly behind her. Main was looking at them with a puzzled expression upon his face. Nowhere could he see aught of his new found friend, but as his eyes fell upon the face of the man seated at the table with Mrs. Bass and Gwendolyn they went wide in consternation, for he recognized at once the features of the crown prince of Karlova whom he had seen pass his hotel that morning in Demia.

"What are you doing here, Mr. Main?" demanded Mrs. Bass.

"I have come to marry Gwendolyn," replied the young man. "You see I have brought a priest with me. Awfully sorry, Mrs. Bass; but I'm bound to have her. I wouldn't have been a party to this thing if it hadn't seemed the only way to save Gwen from a worse fate; but what I can't understand is what his highness is doing here and where my friend The Rider is. Anyway, it's all right; you won't be detained or bothered as soon as Gwen and I are married—I'll see to all that."

"I do not know what you are talking about, Mr. Main," snapped Mrs. Bass; "but unless you are quite mad you will go away at once. His Royal Highness, Prince Boris of Karlova, has honored Gwendolyn with a proposal of marriage; and that is why he sent for this holy man. How you happened to accompany him I can not understand—do you know this person, Prince Boris?"

"Never saw him before," replied The Rider, and then, turning to Main: "You'd better get out of here and get out quick."

Gwendolyn Bass had risen from the table, and now she crossed to Hemmington Main's side.

"Oh, Hemmy," she cried, "don't let them marry me to this awful man."

"You bet your life, I won't," replied Main, and as he spoke he put an arm about her which imparted to Gwendolyn Bass the first sensation of hope and safety which she had experienced in many a long day.

The Rider rose from his chair. His ugly countenance was drawn into a savage scowl. In the breast of his military tunic was the revolver that he could not be persuaded to part with even for an instant. As he advanced upon Hemmington Main he drew the weapons from its hiding place. At sight of it the servants scampered for safety, the priest hopped nimbly out of range, and Mrs. Bass screamed in terror.

Main shoved Gwendolyn quickly to one side lest she be injured should the man fire, and at the same instant drew his own weapon. The two shots blended into a single sharp report as the men pressed the triggers of their weapons simultaneously. The Rider clutched his side and stumbled forward, falling to the floor upon his face. Hemmington Main stood there, white and rigid, looking down upon the fallen man. Gwendolyn Bass cowered, wide-eyed, against the wall, while her mother ran forward to the side of the wounded bandit.

"God help us, Hemmington Main!" cried the older woman, "you have killed the crown prince of Karloval!"

CHAPTER TWELVE

THE Princess Mary stumbled onward and upward through the darkness until it seemed to her that her aching limbs could bear her no farther. At last she stopped.

"You are tired, Miss Bass?" asked her captor.

"I cannot take another step," replied the princess. "Kill me if you will; but I cannot go on."

"And you, Mrs. Bass?" turning to Carlotta.

"I am tired," replied the frightened woman; "but I think I can keep up—maybe I can assist her—er— my daughter."

"No, I'll see to that," said the bandit, and without even a by-your-leave he lifted the princess into his strong arms and resumed the upward scramble.

The girl struggled for a moment to free herself.

"Put me down, please," she commanded in icy tones, "I prefer to walk."

"But you just said that you couldn't take another step," he reminded her, without the slightest indication of any intention to obey her wish. "We can't remain out here all night, you know; and anyway we'll soon be at my camp." He very near added that he wished it was many miles farther, since he had gathered the lithe little form into his arms.

Strands of wavy, soft hair blew now and again against his cheek, and to his nostrils came the delicate aroma of a subtile perfume, such as marks the woman of refinement. The girl's beauty together with the close contact of her warm body aroused in her captor a yearning for that which had always seemed to elude him—one within his own, limited class who might command from him such a love as this girl must command from the young American for whom he had stolen her; one, too, who would give back in equal measure a like love.

The Princess Mary felt the broad bosom against which she was held rise in a deep sigh. She thought the man a most remarkable brigand. She had always heard such frightful tales of the atrocities of The Rider that she had rather expected some show of brutality upon his part, though her judgement had satisfied her that he would offer them no real harm or indignities so long as there remained the hope of obtaining a fat ransom for them. Now she found herself wondering why he sighed—could it be that the fellow had a heart, after all.

"Why," asked the Princess Mary, being as she was rather a creature of impulse—"Why do you sigh?"

The brigand laughed. "I fear," he answered, "that I am, after all, a rather sentimental cutthroat—and you really would like to know why I sighed? Well," and he did not wait for her reply, "I will tell you, though I promise you that you will laugh at me. I was sighing because in all the world from which such as I may choose a love there is no girl like you."

The Princess Mary stiffened and turned her face away. "Put me down at once!" she commanded, and the bandit could not but note the regal haughtiness of her tones. "Put me down, fellow, I shall not be insulted—I can die; but I cannot brook your familiarity."

"You asked me," he reminded her patiently, "why I sighed. I told you merely the truth." There was just a faint trace of levity in his voice, as though he endeavored to suppress a laugh, which aroused still further the ire of the spoiled little princess. She struggled to free herself from his arms; but he only held her the more tightly.

"You can't walk you know," he said; "and we can't sit by the side of the trail forever; so you must let me carry you, and you must not make it difficult. As a matter of fact," he added, as though on second thought, "I can't say that I mind if you do struggle just a little—it makes it necessary for me to hold you just so much tighter."

"You beast!" Her exclamation was a veritable explosion.

"What do you expect of a highwayman?" he asked. "If you were a native, now, of either Margoth or Karlova you would be familiar with the reputation of The Rider and know that you were mighty lucky not to have your ears cut off by this time."

The Princess Mary almost shuddered; but being a brave little princess she didn't, quite. She knew only too well the sinister reputation of The Rider—for the time she had forgotten it in a strange sensation of security which had dominated her almost from the moment that she had fallen into the hands of the bandit—somehow it didn't seem possible that this man could have it in him to harm a defenseless woman. He inspired, in her at least, most inexplicably, a feeling the precise opposite of that which he should have inspired. She could not feel the terror he should have inspired.

Occasionally the man halted to turn back with a courteous word to Carlotta, regretting the fact that he could be of no assistance to her, and inquiring most solicitously how she fared. Poor Carlotta was so terror stricken that she could only mumble incoherent replies, for which the Princess Mary was thankful—the good woman had very nearly divulged their identities already. The princess could not fail to note, though, the courteous deference in the voice of the bandit when he spoke to 'Mrs. Bass,' and her interest in her captor grew accordingly. Could this really be the rough, brutal cutthroat who had terrorized two frontiers for years, who had successfully defied both the gendarmerie and soldiery of two nations, and robbed and murdered at his own sweet will? It was incredible. Why he had the well modulated voice of a cultured gentleman, and he spoke English with that refined precision which marks the use of that language by the educated European a fact which her American education revealed to her.

It was well after midnight when they reached their destination—a little high walled ravine, deep in the mountain fastness of the frontier, and the girl saw before her in the moonlight a rough log shack surrounded by a number of soiled and tattered tents.

A sentry challenged their approach, covering them with his rifle; and at the sound of his voice two score burly ruffians came running from their blankets as though experience had taught them to sleep with their ears wide open and their hands upon their weapons.

"It is I, The Rider," called the man in reply to the challenge.

The sentry lowered his rifle and stepped forward. The others pressed around.

"Get some food for the ladies," commanded the new comer, and then, turning to one of the brigands. "Did a young man come with a priest?"

The fellow addressed shook his head negatively.

"When he does, bring them to me," said The Rider, "and now some of you prepare beds in the shack for the ladies, they are tired after their long climb."

Within the shack a grimy lantern was lighted which scarce relieved the gloom sufficiently to display the filthy squalor of the interior. As he ushered his guests within, The Rider stood in the doorway behind them.

"I am sorry," he said, "that I have no better accommodations to offer you; but by tomorrow I am sure that the very reasonable terms I shall ask for your release will be gladly accepted, and that you will then be able to continue upon your journey to Sovgrad. Food will be brought you, after which you may retire with every confidence that you will not be molested and sleep in as perfect security as though you occupied your own beds at home."

The Rider remained until one of his men had brought some cold meat and a kettle of soup, and lighted a fire in the dilapidated stove which stood precariously upon three legs at one side of the single room of the old building. The light from the lantern gave the Princess Mary her first opportunity to note the features of her captor, and if she had before been struck by the suavity of his speech and the courtesy of his manners she was now doubly impressed by the nobility of his countenance and bearing.

To her surprise she saw before her a young and handsome man upon whose fine features lay no trace of brutality or degeneracy. The mask which had hidden half his face at the moment he had confronted them upon the Roman road he had long since discarded as an uncomfortable nuisance, and he now stood before her with bared head waiting silently for the man to be done with the building of the fire and the heating of the soup, as though loath to leave his prisoners alone with his fellow brigand.

A troubled expression clouded his eyes as another bandit entered with an armful of filthy blankets, which he threw down upon the dirty floor in a corner of the room. He took a step toward the two women.

"I am sorry, Miss Bass," he said, "that you and your mother should be compelled to spend the night in so uncouth and repulsive a place; but I assure you that it cannot now be helped. One whom I expected, and whose presence would have made it possible for you to immediately continue your journey to Sovgrad is not here, and we must await him. Upon his coming and the amiable concurrence of your mother in my plans depends your prompt release—the terms will not be difficult."

"And what, may I ask," demanded the princess, "is the amount of our ransom?"

The light of the lantern played upon the girl's hair and upon her comely features. It revealed the lines of her trim little figure, and the haughty tilt of her royal head which needed no diadem to distinguish it from the heads of ordinary, mortal maids. The Rider had half glimpsed, half guessed the beauty of his younger captive—or at least he had thought that he had; but the revealment of her features in the flickering light of the sordid lantern had left him almost dizzy with the intoxication of the actuality. It was not the beauty of perfection which enthralled him, as it enthralled all who looked upon the Princess Mary of Margoth, for perfection, as measured by the standards of art, was not there. The little nose was a trifle too short, the upper lip a bit too long, the cheek bones just a hair higher than perfection demands, perhaps; but the whole was so moulded, and so animated by that indefinable something which is the essence of beauty that The Rider would have sworn that in all the world there existed no more beautiful woman than this daughter of a plebeian American millionaire, and he sighed because she was promised to another, forgetting for the moment that a still more formidable barrier separated them.

So long he stood in silence looking at the girl that she finally repeated her question, quite peremptorily, and with a little stamp of her foot.

"I asked you, fellow," she said, "the amount of the ransom you demand."

The man who had been working over the stove had cocked an ear when he had heard the girl addressed as Miss Bass, and now he puttered about in an effort to prolong his work in the room that he might learn more of the prisoners and the amount of the ransom. The name was familiar, for the passage of the wife and daughter of Abner J. Bass through almost any civilized country on the globe was heralded broadcast upon the front pages of the newspapers, together with various estimates of the many millions which they represented. The fellow, a stupid lout, could not recall where he had heard the name, yet there was something about it which aroused his attention and held his interest.

The Rider could not repress a smile at the manner in which the girl addressed him, and he hastened to reply, as though always he had been accustomed to obey the haughty commands of an imperious master.

"The ransom," he said "will not be in money. I know that the wife and daughter of Abner J. Bass could command a fabulous sum should I demand it; but I shall not demand a cent of money."

"What shall you demand, then?" asked the princess.

"Something rather more valuable than all the riches of Abner J. Bass," replied the man, and, after a pause,—"the hand of his daughter in marriage."

Both Carlotta and the Princess Mary went white as the full significance of this statement sank into their understandings. The former gave a little scream and moved closer to the princess as though to protect her royal charge from the contaminating touch of the bandit. The princess realized that her plight was a sore one, and that it might be better to conciliate rather than offend her captor.

"You do not understand what you require," she said. "It is absolutely impossible that you and I should wed. Name a ransom that may be paid in money, and it will be paid gladly; but do not lose all by attempting to force such preposterous terms upon us."

"Wait!" said The Rider. "You do not understand. I am not asking your hand for myself; but for another whom I understand you would gladly wed would your mother permit. Your freedom, therefore, depends upon my ability to obtain from her the necessary consent to your immediate marriage to Mr.

Hemmington Main, who is on his way here now with a priest who will perform the ceremony."

Then The Rider looked eagerly from one to the other for evidence of the expected effect of his announcement. The girl should have been quite overcome by joy; but she was not. She appeared, on the contrary, far from relieved and even a little piqued. Could it be that the Princess Mary of Margoth was, after all, angered to discover that the bandit had not wanted her for himself at all, but for another? Impossible, and yet a princess is, whether she will or no, a woman; and Prince Boris of Karlova, even in the guise of a notorious cutthroat, was a most prepossessing figure.

The bandit at the stove gasped as he heard the terms of the ransom and learned the identity of the captives. A cunning expression crossed his stupid face, as, satisfied with what he had heard, he slunk from the building and hastened to the tents of his fellows to communicate his store of intelligence.

"You have made a mistake," said the princess. "I do not wish to marry Mr. Main, and as you say that you have no wish for a money ransom may I ask you to return us to our car and let us go our way?"

The Rider showed his astonishment in the expression of his face.

"But," he insisted, "I have Mr. Main's word for it that you and your father are in favor of the match— that only your mother's wish that you marry a titled European stands in the way." He turned questioningly toward Carlotta.

"Her hi—er—my daughter," stammered the frightened nurse, "can marry only a titled European—it is
her wish as well as my own. She does not wish to
marry Mr. Main—you have heard her say so yourself. Please, oh, please, Mr. Rider, let us go."

The Rider rubbed his chin in puzzled bewilder-
ment. Whatever his reply to Carlotta's appeal might
have been it was interrupted by the sound of the
approach of several men the foremost of whom burst
into the shack with scant formality. The leader was a
burly brute whose gaudy rags were rendered sinister
by a bandoleer of cartridges across his breast and a
formidable looking rifle which he carried in his right
hand. He halted just within the doorway and eyed
The Rider with a ferocious scowl. The latter's head
went up, and a scowl of disapproval darkened his
brow.

"What is the meaning of this?" he asked. "I did not
send for you."

"No," growled the brigand, "you didn't send for
me; but I came—I came to tell you that you don't let
these fine birds get away so easy as you think. Why,
we could get a million for 'em; an' here you are tellin'
'em they can go if the young one will marry the man
you want her to. What do you think we are, to stand
around an' let you lose the richest pickin's we've had
in years?"

"Get out of here," snapped The Rider.

"Hold on now, my fine bird," cried the brigand.
"We've promised not to do you no harm, an' we
won't unless you make us; but we're goin' to have

these two women, an' we're goin' to take 'em with us right now; so stand aside and you won't get hurt," and the fellow took a step as though to pass Prince Boris.

Carlotta shrank close to Princess Mary, who put her arms about her faithful servant and stood waiting the outcome of the altercation with calm and unruffled demeanor. The girl had heard the words of the brigand with surprise, and though she still had no reason to doubt the identity of him whom she took for The Rider she wondered not a little at the temerity and the mutinous spirit of his subordinates.

As the ruffian attempted to pass him Prince Boris took a single step forward, and at the same instant swung his fist to the fellow's jaw, delivering a blow that stretched the man upon his back. Those in the doorway behind now attempted to surge into the room; but Boris drew his revolver and menaced them as they advanced. The man upon the floor, cursing and sputtering in pain and rage, staggered to his feet. In an instant his rifle was leveled.

"I don't care who you are," he shrieked, with a horrid oath, "you can't come that on me and live," but before he could press the trigger there was a spurt of flame from the revolver in the hand of Prince Boris and the man, dropping his rifle, staggered forward, reeled and fell at the feet of the prince he would have slain.

Some one of the men in the doorway fired a shot into the room, and instantly Boris' revolver spurted a streak of fire and death into the group huddled there.

One of the bandits screamed and fell backwards into the arms of those behind him. Boris fired again, and the pack fled, carrying their wounded with them.

Leaping to the door the crown prince of Karlova closed and barred it, then he turned back to the two women.

"Lie down close behind the chimney," he commanded. "Their bullets are less apt to find you there. Quick, now! They will be back in a minute—you are too rich spoil for them to relinquish without a battle."

He stepped to the smoky lantern and raising it extinguished the flame, leaving the room in utter darkness. Then he went to the side of the dead brigand, removed his bandoleer of cartridges, which he buckled about his own shoulders, and appropriated the fellow's revolver and rifle.

"We can give them a fight for a while," he said, with a laugh.

"Why don't you let them take us for ransom?" asked Princess Mary. "They may kill us all."

"They are beasts," replied Boris. "I would rather see you dead than alone in their power. If the ransom were all, I might make terms with them; though if it were not for you I'd rather take a chance with their bullets than give in to them."

He had crossed to one of the two windows as he spoke; and an instant later a shot from his rifle crashed through the glass, announcing that he had discovered the enemy sneaking upon their little fortress.

"I think I got another of them that time," he remarked, and then crossed the room to the window upon the opposite side. Again the report of his rifle crashed through the small room.

"They're coming from both directions," he announced. I wish Main had come—two of us might stand them off for a while."

As he recrossed the room to the opposite window he felt the touch of a light hand upon his arm.

"Give me a revolver," said a brave little voice at his side. "I can guard upon one side, while you guard upon the other."

A sudden volley of shots from without shattered the glass in one of the windows and thudded against the logs of the walls. A bullet pinged close to the man's head. Involuntarily he threw his arm about the girl beside him and forced her to the floor.

"You mustn't take such chances," he exclaimed. "My God, they might have hit you." His fingers closed tightly upon her arm, and the contact sent a thrill through the man's frame. "Go back to the chimney," he said, hoarsely. "May God forgive me for exposing you to this danger, for I can never forgive myself."

"You are a most remarkable brigand," said the girl; "your actions belie your reputation. Are you always as solicitous of the welfare of your victims?"

Prince Boris laughed. "I am rather beginning to believe," he said, "that I am a remarkable brigand," and then, seriously, "I never before captured a goddess."

The Princess Mary rose and shook his hand from her arm.

"I will guard this window," she said; "you take the other. There is no use objecting, we shall all be killed if we do otherwise," and she crossed the room to one of the windows, where she fired out upon the figures creeping through the brush toward the shack.

"Be careful!" he called back to her over his shoulder, and then, quite irreverently, "Why couldn't you have been a European princess instead of an American queen!"

CHAPTER THIRTEEN

THE bandits had now settled down to a determined siege. The bullets were thudding against the walls or entering the windows with a business-like regularity which reflected the inflexible purpose of the attackers. It was only occasionally that Boris could find in the flash of a gun even a fair target for a return shot, and he would not waste his precious supply of ammunition without some likelihood of a hit.

The girl, upon her side of the room, fired with equal care and coolness; and as the man heard the report of her rrvolver from time to time something stirred in his heart which no woman ever had stirred before.

"Ah," he thought, "what a queen she would make!"

And the girl, oblivious alike of his thoughts and his identity, found herself regretting that he was but an unhung outlaw.

Presently there was a lull in the firing, and a voice bellowed out of the darkness, demanding that they surrender and promising freedom for the man and a fair ransom for the two women.

The replies of both the man and the girl were identical and simultaneous. Two shots rang out from the interior of the shack as the voice of the brigand ceased, and immediately the battle recommenced with increased violence. As the bullets shattered the few remaining remnants of splintered glass from the window panes the girl crawled across the floor to the man's side.

"Give me some more ammunition," she whispered. "I have used all that was in that belt."

He turned and placed a hand upon hers where it rested on his arm.

"Go over to the chimney and hide," he replied; "I have no more revolver ammunition—and only a few more rounds for the rifle."

She made no move to obey him, nor did she remove her hand from beneath his.

"Hurry," he said; "you might be shot here—uselessly."

"You are very brave," said the Princess Mary. "I do not understand why you, The Rider, should risk your life in battle with your own men to protect me."

The man leaned closer to her. From the darkness of the night without came a sullen roar as the brigands, sensing the diminution of the firing from within, rose to rush the shack.

"It can do no harm to tell you now," he said, "for

death is very near, for me at least—there was a reason which was based on honor; but had that reason not existed there is another which would have made it a joy for me to give my life for you—would you like to hear it?"

And though the Princess Mary of Margoth knew the words that he was about to speak, and though she knew him for a brutal robber, for an outcast, for a pariah, she whispered: "Yes."

"Because I love you," he said, and raised her fingers to his lips.

And then a volley rattled loudly about them, he pushed her to the floor in the shelter of the log wall, and, rising, fired upon the charging ruffians without.

On they came, though some fell, until they battered at the door with their gun butts; smashed at the sturdy timbers that at last splintered and gave, while within the dark interior Prince Boris of Karlova stood with hot rifle pumping his remaining cartridges through the panels into the cursing, screaming mob without.

The door was swinging in upon its broken hinges when, of a sudden, there came a sharp volley from the edge of the ravine, a volley which was followed by the clear, piercing strains of a bugle sounding The Charge!

Mary of Margoth leaped to her feet.

"The Guard!" she cried. "Stefan carried the word to Demia, and The Guard has come!"

A moment later the brigands were fleeing before the shots of the royal troopers; and as an officer stepped into the interior of the little room, a flash lamp in his hand, he saw a tall young man standing in the middle of the floor, an empty rifle dangling in his right hand and blood flowing down the side of his face from a flesh wound across his temple. Behind the young man stood a much dishevelled girl, and as the eyes of the captain crossed to her he sprang forward, and going upon one knee raised the girl's fingers to his lips, with a fervent: "Thank God that Your Royal Highness in unharmed."

Boris of Karlova turned wide and wondering eyes upon the tableau at his side. "Your Royal Highness," he muttered to himself, and then other officers and troopers pushed into the room, in their midst a bloody and ragged prisoner.

"There he is," shouted the prisoner. "There he is! There's the man your lookin' for—The Rider!" and he pointed a grimy forefinger at Prince Boris of Karlova. "An' I want the reward that's been upon his head these many years."

The officers pressed forward to sieze the renowned bandit, and at the same time Princess Mary of Margoth stepped between them and their prey.

"Wait!" she said. "He is indeed The Rider; but this night he has won the gratitude of Margoth, for at the risk of his life he has fought for me and saved me from these ruffians. Let him go Captain."

"Who are you?" asked Boris of Karlova, turning wondering eyes upon the girl. "I thought that you were Miss Bass the American."

"I am Mary, Princess of Margoth," she replied;

"and—I am your friend, too, no matter what or who you are."

"I am sorry, your highness," interrupted Captain Polnik; "but I must place this man under arrest and take him back to Demia. Upon his hands is the blood of many innocent victims. He is a menace to the safety of the roads and to the people of Margoth. His defense of your highness will doubtless win him the clemency of the court before which he must be tried for his crimes; so that instead of expiating those crimes upon the gibbet he may hope for the lesser punishment of imprisonment for life."

Boris of Karlova gave a long whistle. Imprisonment for life! Of course by divulging his identity he could escape all that; but the scandal! No! he dared not tell them who he was—he must wait and find a better way out of his difficulty, and so it was that the crown prince of Karlova was led back to the capitol city of Margoth and thrown into prison within sight of the palace where the Princess Mary took with unwonted meekness a severe lecture from her royal sire.

CHAPTER FOURTEEN

As THE true Rider dropped to the shot from Hemmington Main's revolver, the terrified priest, seeing in his own presence upon the scene of the crime, a sufficient evidence to implicate him in the assassination of the crown prince, slunk from the lodge, mounted his horse and galloped madly toward Sovgrad.

On the floor of the breakfast room he had just quitted Mrs. Abner J. Bass and two servants kneeled over the prostrate form of the wounded man. Hemmington Main stood where he had when he had fired the shot, and now Gwendolyn Bass crossed the room and took her place at his side, laying a trembling hand upon his arm.

"O, Hemmy," she whispered, "what will they do to you? It is awful!"

"I don't care what they do to me," he replied miserably. "They'll probably hang me eventually; but it's worth it to have saved you from such a fate," and he motioned toward the man upon the floor, a grimace of disgust accompanying the gesture.

Mrs. Bass turned toward them. "He lives," she said; "it may not be a fatal wound, after all. Heaven grant that it is not."

As she spoke two men entered the neglected doorway of the royal hunting lodge, saw the group in the breakfast room, and entered. One was a low browed, evil looking fellow; the other a red faced, well fed priest. The former was the first to speak and announce their presence to the tense, pre-occupied actors in the little tragedy upon which they had burst.

"Wot's here?" he demanded, crossing to the side of the wounded bandit.

"Prince Boris has been shot," said Mrs. Bass. "It was accidental. Some one must go for a physician at once."

The man looked quickly about at the others in the room as he heard The Rider described as Prince Boris. No one contradicted or corrected Mrs. Bass. Then one of the servants spoke up.

"The priest who was here has, I think, gone for help," he said. "He mounted and rode away in the direction of Sovgrad immediately after the—ah—accident. Doubtless he will inform the palace officials," and he looked meaningly at the low browed new comer.

"How bad is he hurt?" asked the fellow.

Mrs. Bass shook her head. "I do not know—he is still unconscious."

The man thought for a moment; then he turned to the priest who had accompanied him. "We've got to get him away from here," he said.

The priest nodded. The servants seemed relieved. The Americans could not but wonder at the heartless apathy of the royal retainers. No word of regret at the shooting of their prince had passed the lips of any of them, nor a single menace for the man who had shot him.

At the command of the priest's companion two of the servants lifted the unconscious man and carried him from the lodge where they placed him in the arms of the low browed one, who had preceded them and mounted his horse in readiness to receive the 'prince.' The priest meanwhile clambered laboriously into his own saddle, and presently the trio were lost to sight in the darkness.

The Americans, who had come to the verandah to watch the departure of the silent, mysterious company, now returned to the interior of the building, the royal servants following them. Mrs. Bass turned toward Hemmington Main.

"Hemmington," she said; "we are in a frightful predicament. At any moment they come from Sovgrad. What are we to do? You have blasted what was, a few moments ago, my dearest ambition. I should feel resentment and anger; but I do not. Something, perhaps the shock of this unexpected tragedy, seems to have awakened me to a realization of the foolishness, yes, and the wickedness of the thing I was attempting to force Gwendolyn into. It has taught me how great your love for my daughter must be, that you would willingly face the consequences of an attack upon a prince in his own country to protect her from him and from me and save her from an unholy union in which it is impossible that there could have been love upon either side.

"I realize that the fault is all mine, Hemmington; but the thing is done now and cannot be undone. All we can do is to work together to save you from the consequences of my foolishness. There is a motor car outside, and the Margothian border lies but a few miles to the east."

Hemmington Main could not have been more surprised if the king of Karlova had ridden up and decorated him for shooting the crown prince. But though he felt his astonishment there was no time now to waste in useless expressions of surprise or thankfulness. He turned toward the servants—would they attempt to detain him? Unquestionably they would. As far as he could discover none of them was armed. Hemmington Main placed himself between the women and the servants; then he drew his revolver and covered the latter.

"Go out to the car," he said to Mrs. Bass and her daughter, and then to the servants: "If you give an alarm or attempt to prevent our escape you'll get precisely what your royal master got."

The oldest of the servants, a venerable looking butler with the mein and dignity of a Roman emperor, permitted his face to relax into as near the semblance of a smile as his atrophied muscles would permit.

"You need have no fear, monsieur," he said, "that we shall attempt to detain you. Nothing would suit us better than to have you safely across the border into Margoth should it happen that the crazy priest has really gone to the palace with the story of what transpired here tonight. Then, surely, we shall have enough to explain without having to explain you and these two ladies."

The American evidently revealed his incredulity of the man's sincerity in the expression of his face following the butler's words, for the latter hastened to reassure him.

"There is much in this matter which you do not understand, and which I may not divulge; but I give you my word, monsieur, that His Royal Highness, Prince Boris of Karlova, will reward me well if I succeed in getting you out of Karlova before you fall into the hands of the officers of the king, his father."

"No," said Hemmington Main, "I don't understand; but I'm willing to take your word for it so long as you'll all remain indoors until we are well upon our way."

"Certainly, monsieur," replied the servant. "Good night, monsieur, and good luck!"

"Good night," said Hemmington Main, and waving the two women toward the doorway he backed out of the room and passed forever from the royal hunting lodge of the crown prince of Karlova.

The limousine stood in the driveway, the royal chauffeur was at the wheel. Main helped Mrs. Bass and her daughter into the tonneau, and then took the seat beside the driver.

"To Demia," he said, "and let her out."

CHAPTER FIFTEEN

As Hemmington Main entered the dining room of the hotel at Demia the following morning he opened a morning paper which he had just purchased in the lobby. Vying with one another for importance were two news items upon the first page. One reported the abduction of Princess Mary of Margoth by the notorious Rider, and her subsequent rescue by the royal troops. Main whistled as he read of the capture of the famous bandit and the probable fate which was in store for him.

"Such a prize tempted him from fulfilling his little promise to me," thought Main; "though how in sin the thing got so balled up I can't imagine. His note to Peter certainly resulted in my being led to Gwendolyn—I can't understand it."

Further along in the account of the occurrence

was another item which brought a second whistle to the lips of the American.

"Princess Mary," it read, "insists that The Rider did not know her true identity until after the royal troops had rescued her and captured the brigand. He appeared to believe that she was the daughter of Abner J. Bass, the American millionaire, and that the lady in waiting who accompanied her was Mrs. Bass. An element of mystery surrounds the entire adventure, and is still further augmented by the connection which is seen between the abduction of Princess Mary and the reported assassination of Prince Boris of Karlova, the details of which appear in another column of this paper, for in the latter tragedy the names of Mrs. Bass and her daughter also appear, as well as that of Hemmington Main, an American newspaper man."

There was an excellent reproduction of Klopkoi's famous portrait of Mary of Margoth, beneath which was a tribute of love and devotion to "Our Little Princess, the last of the Banatoffs."

The account of the reported assassination of the crown prince of Karlova was most carefully worded, and showed the hand of the censor in every line. The account closed with these words: "It is not yet definitely known if the prince be really dead, for following the tragedy he was spirited away by unknown accomplices of the conspirators. The servants at the royal hunting lodge deny that Prince Boris was there last night, or that he was shot; but the priest who reported the affair swears that he saw him with his own eyes and that he saw the shot fired which killed him. The authorities, it is reported, found blood upon a large Persian rug in the breakfast room, at the very spot where the priest says the prince fell, mortally wounded. The prefect of police at Demia has been asked to detain and question all strangers, especially Americans, now in the capitol. Margoth is anxious to demonstrate her friendship and sympathy for Karlova by cooperating with her in every way in the apprehension and arrest of the conspirators."

Mr. Main's whistle became a long and heartfelt thing as he assimilated the full purport of that last paragraph. He was still staring intently at the article when Gwendolyn Bass entered the dining room, and seeing him, crossed the room to his table.

"Good morning Hemmy," she said. "Isn't it good to be safe and sound in Demia after all the horrid adventures of yesterday?"

"Yes," he replied mournfully, "we're so awfully 'safe and sound'—look at this," and he passed the paper over to her, holding a forefinger on the paragraph which had caused his perturbation.

Miss Bass read the article through. Then her eyes wandered to the portrait of the Princess Mary and opened in astonished wonderment.

" 'Princess Mary,' " she quoted, and " 'the last of the Banatoffs'—why Hemmington Main this is little Mary Banatoff who roomed with me at college. She called on me here last evening, and I never knew she was a princess."

Main rose excitedly and leaned across the table to look once more at the picture of the princess as though the evidence of his own eyes would substantiate that of his companion's, though he had never seen either Mary Banatoff or the Princess Mary of Margoth.

"Why, Gwen!" he cried. "Are you sure?"

"As sure as I am that I know your face, Hemmy," she replied.

A shadow fell across the table where the two bent over the likeness of the Margothian princess. Thinking that the waiter had come for their orders, Main looked up to behold a large, scowling gentleman gorgeous in gold lace and braid. Behind him stood a file of gendarmes.

"Monsieur Main?" asked the officer.

The American nodded.

"And Mademoiselle Bass?"

Again Main assented.

"Come with me," said the officer; "you are under arrest."

"Eh?" ejaculated Main.

"It is quite true, monsieur," replied the other; "and it would be well to come without a scene."

The American plead with the officer to permit Miss Bass to remain at the hotel; but the man was politely firm, explaining that he but acted upon the orders of a superior.

"But at least you will let her communicate with her mother?" he asked.

"Oh, yes, she will have an opportunity to communicate with her mother," replied the officer, and when the party reached the lobby of the hotel Main discovered the explanation of the man's generosity—Mrs. Bass was there awaiting them—she, too, was under arrest.

It was a melancholy party that drove to the gloomy portals of Demia's gaol, likewise a silent party for their guardians would permit no conversation between the prisoners. Main still clutched the morning paper in his hand, and as he gazed vacantly at it the features of Margoth's girlish princess smiled up at him from the blur of type. An inspiration seized him. The Princess Mary was a friend of Gwen's. If Gwen could only see her and explain, surely everything would be set right so far as Gwen and her mother were concerned. He of course would have to pay the penalty for the shooting of Prince Boris—the pig! He asked permission to say half a dozen words to his fellow prisoner, but the guard silenced him with a curt word and a menacing shake of a baton.

They were slowing up now before the jail, and Main was at his wits ends to find a way to communicate with Gwendolyn Bass. She had risen to leave the car which had transported them from the hotel when Main seized upon the only plan that seemed at all feasible for communicating with her. Taking a pencil from his pocket he wrote across the picture of the princess: "See her," and as Gwendolyn Bass passed him to leave the car he pushed the paper into her hands.

CHAPTER SIXTEEN

A few minutes later, after having been carefully searched, Main was conducted to a dark cell below the street level. The door clanged behind him, the turnkey shuffled away; and, so far as his eyes could penetrate the unaccustomed darkness, the American was alone.

But he had taken but a single turn of his tiny cell when a pleasant voice broke the silence of the prison —a voice which came from close at hand through the grating which separated Main's cell from that adjoining it upon the left.

"Ah, my good friend the American joker!" exclaimed the voice. "But the joke seems also to be upon the joker, eh?"

Main stepped to the grating and peered through.

His eyes, becoming accustomed to the darkness, presently discovered a familiar figure reclining at ease upon the hard wooden bench.

"Joker!" ejaculated Main. "You, my friend, are the prince of jokers; and this is the result of your pleasantry."

The other was silent for a moment. "What is beyond me," he said presently, "is how in the world you obtained the connivance of the royal chauffeur and even of the princess herself and her companion— none of them denied that they were the Basses."

"I don't understand you," said Main. "I obtained the connivance of no one. Mrs. Bass and her daughter left Demia as I told you they would; but instead of being waylaid by you as we had arranged, they fell in some way into the hands of Prince Boris of Karlova. The note you gave me to Peter the innkeeper resulted in my being taken to the hunting lodge of the prince, where I found Miss Bass, her mother and prince Boris—the latter was about to wed Miss Bass. It was in the altercation over this that he was shot."

The man in the adjoining cell leaped to his feet. "Shot?" he cried.

"Yes, I shot him in self defense—that is why I am here. Miss Bass and her mother are prisoners, too. Haven't you seen the papers? Didn't you know that they report the assassination of the crown prince of Karlova and the secret removal of his body from the lodge?"

"Well!" ejaculated M. Kargovitch; "you certainly

have gotten into a devil of a muss—and you really didn't have anything to do with my getting hold of Princess Mary instead of Miss Bass?"

"Upon my word of honor," replied Hemmington Main.

"Then we are the victims of the strangest combination of circumstances it has been my ill fortune to experience," said M. Kargovitch; "and I give you my word of honor, monsieur, that I honestly thought I was waylaying your American friends and helping you in your little affair of the heart. The note I gave you should have resulted in your being brought to where I awaited you. Why, I even went so far as to demand from the lady in waiting who accompanied her highness that she give her consent to the marriage of Mary of Margoth to Mr. Hemmington Main of New York," and M. Kargovitch leaned back against the steel bars of his cell and laughed heartily.

"You take things rather easily for a man who will probably make the acquaintance of a gibbet in a few days," said Main, laughingly. "Do you know, my friend, that you are a mighty good sport? I only wish that I might help you some way."

"You would laugh, too, Main, if you knew as much about certain matters as do I," replied Kargovitch. "You think that I will be hanged as a brigand, but I won't. You also think that you will be hanged for assassinating a prince of the blood-royal but you won't."

"Well," said Main, "I hope you know what you are talking about."

A door opened at the far end of the corridor as he spoke, and with the clanking of sabers a party of officers and soldiers approached the cells in which the two men were confined. They halted before that occupied by M. Kargovitch. An officer drew a formidable appearing document from the breast of his tunic, and as he unfolded it a soldier bearing a lighted lantern held it so that the rays of light fell upon the paper.

As he read in sonorous tones the solemn and formal words of a long preamble which recited the career of crime of one individual known only as The Rider the smile broadened upon the face of M. Kargovitch; but at the last paragraph it died, the man's head went up haughtily, and though he paled his shoulders remained squared, nor did he give any outward sign of what might be passing in his breast.

For the paper concluded: "And so, through the clemency of His Gracious Majesty, Alexis III, King of Margoth, it is decreed that said The Rider shall not expiate his sins upon the scaffold as custom and the laws decree, but shall, instead be granted the more honorable death before a firing squad of the king's soldiers at dawn upon the morrow."

And having completed the reading the officers and soldiers turned and tramped away down the corridor, their footsteps resounding dismally through the gloomy prison vault.

It was several minutes after they had departed before either of the prisoners spoke. The Karlovian stood as they had left him, his shoulders squared, his chin up, staring straight before him. Hemmington Main was dumfounded. The other's assurance had been so great just prior to the coming of the soldiers that even now the American could scarce believe that he really had heard read the death warrant of his fellow prisoner. He raised his eyes to the man's face to note the effect of the announcement upon him. M. Kargovitch seemed to feel the American's gaze for he turned slowly toward Main, and as he did so a smile spread across his face.

"If I recall correctly," he said, "your last remark, before they came, was to the effect that you hoped I knew what I was talking about. You see now, don't you, that I did know. I told you that I should not be hanged. Well, I shall not be hanged—they are going to shoot me."

"I wonder," mused Hemmington Main, "if your gift of prophesy will prove as painfully inspired in my case as it has in yours."

M. Kargovitch laughed. "I have it in my power, my friend, to save us both," he said; "but at a cost against which the lives of two men are as nothing, for should I speak now it would throw Margoth and Karlova into bloody war. Alexis of Margoth could scarce overlook the double affront and injury which I have put upon his daughter; and could he, the people of Margoth could not. They worship her, nor, since I have seen her, do I wonder.

"If, through the American minister, you can obtain a sufficient stay the truth must eventually come out, and with the truth known you will be freed from the accusation of having attempted the life of Prince Boris of Karlova."

"If the truth is bound to be known," suggested Main, "why the devil don't you divulge it now and save your own life?"

M. Kargovitch shrugged. "There are several things worse than death, at least to a man in my position. One of them is ridicule. I have made a fool of myself; and I should be laughed at—deservedly. I could not endure it. There is another reason. Within the past two days I have been a party to a hideous hoax, the entire brunt of which fell upon a defenseless girl. I would almost as lief die as look her in the face again, for, inexplicable irony of fate, I have found that I love her."

Hemmington Main, his head tilted to one side, looked quizzically through narrowed lids at his fellow prisoner.

"I can't fathom you, Kargovitch," he said. "You are certainly the most remarkable brigand the world has ever produced."

"Yes," replied Kargovitch, "I am a remarkable brigand. As a matter of fact, Main, I rather suspect that the Lord never intended me for a brigand at all."

In a little back room in the attic of Peter's Inn a man tossed feverishly upon a pile of grimy quilts and blankets. Above him bent a bewhiskered little man whom two others in the room addressed as "Doctor."

"He will live," announced the man of medicine, "if he has proper nursing."

"Bakla will look after him well," said Peter. "Eh, Bakla?"

"Yes," replied the girl, "I will take care of him."

Peter and the doctor left the room, stumping down the rickety ladder which led to the floor below, and the girl took her place upon an upturned keg near the sick man's head, that she might change the cold cloths upon his burning forehead.

An hour passed. The man's mutterings and tossing ceased. He opened his eyes in which now shown the light of rationality.

"Bakla," he exclaimed. "What has happened? What am I doing here?" And then, before she could reply: "Ah, yes; I remember. The American. He shot me. Have you heard anything? Have the papers come yet from Sovgrad? I should like to hear what they have to say, and also what Prince Boris says. I should like to learn how he has explained the thing. I am glad, Bakla, that I am a brigand and not a prince. Go down and fetch the papers, Bakla, will you?"

The girl renewed the cloth upon The Rider's head and descended the ladder to the second floor from which she ran down to the bar room. The Sovgrad papers, still unopened, lay upon a table near the door. She gathered them all up and returned to her patient. They laughed together over the guarded announcement of the reported assassination of the crown prince, and of the strange disappearance of his body. Then Bakla read of the capture of The

Rider by the soldiers of Margoth and the probable fate which awaited him in Demia.

The Rider whistled and looked solemn. "That will never do," he said, "he is a real man, even if he is a prince—far too good a man to make the acquaintance of a rope's end."

"You think they would hang him?" almost screamed Bakla.

"They might," replied The Rider. "They would not believe him should he say he was Prince Boris of Karlova—no, they would only laugh at him, for did they not see me in Demia only yesterday and vouched for as the crown prince of Karlova?"

"But his friends—they know the truth?" persisted Bakla.

"I wonder if they do," mused The Rider. "The whole thing has been so terribly tangled and confused that it is possible they might really believe that it is the true Rider who lies in prison at Demia, and that Prince Boris, who was to have met me at his hunting lodge today, arrived there ahead of time and was actually the man who was shot by the American. They would be none too loath to have me out of the way, for if their connection with this affair becomes known they will probably suffer degradation and imprisonment. Oh, the devil take that American! He has put me in a fix which won't let me do a thing."

Bakla sat in silence for a long while. Her eyes were very wide, and fear-filled. Presently The Rider slept. His regular breathing denoted the deep and healing slumber which is Nature's greatest remedy. The girl rose and tiptoed to the head of the ladder. Quietly she descended. Tillie was busy with the house work on the second floor.

"Listen for The Rider," said Bakla to her. "If he calls, go to him. I am going to Sovgrad. I will be back as quickly as possible."

Tillie would have interposed objections but the girl was gone before she could frame or voice them. A few minutes later, astride a tall, lanky roan who knew the highways of the border better by night than by day, she was riding at a rapid gallop toward Sovgrad.

In time to the drumming hoof beats of the great horse Bakla droned, over and over: "They're goin' to hang Dimmie! They're goin' to hang Dimmie! They're goin' to hang Dimmie!" and the horror in her eyes increased to the inborne suggestion of the hideous thought.

Prince Boris of Karlova spent a long and weary day in the prison at Demia. Early in the afternoon an officer had come and taken the American away without explanation. Boris wondered if they were going to shoot him, too, or if he had been extradited to Karlova, which was the more probable.

As a matter of fact Hemmington Main had been conducted to the palace, led to the second floor, and ushered, without a word of explanation, into the presence of three women. Two he recognized at once —Mrs. Bass and Gwendolyn, and a moment later he was presented to the third, and found himself bowing very low over the hand of Princess Mary of Margoth.

"It was the suggestion you wrote across Her Highness's picture this morning which resulted in our being freed in less than half an hour," explained Gwendolyn Bass; "but for the longest time nothing could be done for you. His majesty could not be prevailed upon to release you, even though we all offered to vouch for your presence when ever you were wanted. He was awfully nice and kind about it all, but you see you are a very important prisoner, and he could take no chance of offending Karlova by seeming to look lightly upon your offense."

"Well, how did you accomplish it then?" asked Main. "I don't seem to be very rigidly imprisoned now."

"We don't know what happened to change my father's mind," said the princess. "All we know is that a few minutes since M. Klein came to announce that you were to be liberated, and I asked that you be brought directly here."

"Well," said Hemmington Main, "it beats me. I wish some good angel might intercede for my fellow prisoner. He seems an awfully good sort—not at all the kind one would take for a brigand, and he's so brave in the face of the fact that he is to die at dawn."

"Die at dawn?" cried Princess Mary of Margoth. "Die at dawn? What do you mean?"

"I heard them read his sentence just a short time before I was liberated—he is to be shot in the morning, poor fellow. And do you know," continued the

American, "there's a mighty pathetic side to it. It seems that he has it within his power to save himself; but pride and honor are keeping his lips sealed. There's something about a girl he has fallen in love with—I couldn't make out just what it was all about —but he's offended her in some way and would rather die than let her know the truth. Foolish of course; but none the less courageous and chivalrous. I tell you, that fellow, highwayman or no highwayman, is a real man—every inch of him."

Princess Mary of Margoth was standing with her back to a window, so it is probable that none of her guests noticed that her face went from white to red and back to white again several times during Hemmington Main's recital, or saw the moisture which gathered in her eyes, fight as she would to keep it back. A moment later she withdrew from the apartment, after summoning a lady-in-waiting and arranging for the comfort and entertainment of her American friends.

The king was seated in his cabinet, when, as was her custom, the Princess Mary entered unannounced. Prince Stroebel was there, too, and Baron Kantchi, the Karlovian minister, with a very tall young man in the uniform of The Black Guard.

They all rose as she entered the room; but she passed among them straight to the king as though she did not see them. Her eyes were very wide, and in them was a look of pain and terror that Alexis III had never seen there during all the short life of his little daughter.

"Mary!" he said, "What has happened?"

"I have just heard," she said in a dull voice, "that you are going to have him shot tomorrow morning. It is a wicked thing and must not be done!"

"You mean," exclaimed the king, "that you have come here to intercede for the life of the notorious Rider—confessed cutthroat and ruffian?"

"He is a brave man," cried the princess. "He fought for me, and saved me, possibly, from worse than death. He deserves better at your hands."

"He is a criminal of the lowest type," expostulated Alexis III. "He is a menace to society. The world will be better for his death."

"I do not believe that he is bad at heart," insisted the girl. "To me and to Carlotta he was all that a noble and chivalrous gentleman should be. Imprison him if you must; but do not have him shot!"

"My daughter," said the king, kindly but firmly, "The Rider should be hanged; but in the indictment and sentence which was recently read to the prisoner we explained that his honorable treatment of our daughter had won him our clemency—therefore he will be shot rather than hanged. No one could ask for more for The Rider—even for you I can grant him no more."

"Oh, Da-da!" cried the girl, and there was a choking sob in her voice. "Please! Please!"

But the king only took her by the hand and led her from the room, shaking his head sadly.

CHAPTER SEVENTEEN

PRINCE BORIS paced back and forth the narrow limits of his cell. He had discovered that by standing with his back against the bars at one side three equal paces should bring his boot in contact with the bars upon the opposite side. After a little practice he was able to measure his strides so accurately that with eyes closed he could take the three steps, and on the third have the toe of his boot just touching the bars. It was not an exciting form of diversion; but it was better than nothing and fully as profitable as counting the upright bars which formed three sides of his cell. He was engaged in this thrilling pastime when the door at the end of the corridor opened once again.

Prince Boris halted and strained his eyes through the darkness. He welcomed the break in the monotony of his solitary confinement, and wondered who the visitor might be and what his errand. There was but a single individual, whose light foot falls caused scarcely a reverberation in the dismal corridor. As the new comer approached Boris saw a small figure wrapped in a long, dark cloak.

"An assassin with a dagger," mused Prince Boris, with a grin. "I would welcome him none the less, though. The devil would be better company than none."

Now the little figure stopped before his cell, and threw back the hood which had covered its head and face. At sight of the latter Prince Boris of Karlova gave a gasp of astonishment and delight.

"Your Highness!" he cried.

The girl looked up into his face, so far above hers. She was very white, and Boris could see that it was with difficulty that she composed herself. "What in the world brings you to this place?" he asked.

"Mr. Main has told me that you might free yourself if you would," she replied, "and I have come to beg of you to speak—to tell them the thing that will liberate you, no matter how it may affect any other. I have done my best to save you; but I can do nothing —nothing. My father, the king, is determined that you shall die. Tell me, O tell me, what it is that you know which would gain your freedom for you."

"I cannot understand," he said, "what has brought your highness here other than a sense of honorable gratitude to one who deserves nothing but your scorn and contempt. I don't wish to die; but I could face death, your highness, rather than tell you the thing you ask to know. I have been a fool; but I am not entirely without a sense of honor."

His hands gripped the iron bars which separated them. His face was pressed close in an interstice between two cold, steel rods. The Princess Mary stepped impulsively closer. She laid her two warm little hands upon his, sending a thrill tingling through every fiber of his being; but when she tried to say the thing that trembled upon her lips, she hesitated, stammered, and dropped her eyes to the rough flagging of the floor.

"What is it?" he whispered. "What do you wish to say to The Rider?"

"Oh, it is so hard," she cried. "Hard, because I am what I am. Were I just a girl I might find the courage to say what I want to say; but I am a princess, muzzled, fettered and constrained by ages of hereditary pride, by silly etiquette, and senseless customs."

Gently he laid one of his hands upon hers.

"Do not say it then," he said "I would not for the world have you suffer even the slightest embarrassment on my account. Remember, your highness, who and what I am."

"I will say it!" she cried. "Last night, just before The Guard came, when you thought that death was very near, you told me that you loved me." She stumbled pitifully over the last three words. "If you spoke the truth then, you will speak the truth now and say the words that will free you, because— because—Oh, God have mercy on my soul!—I—love —you!"

Prince Boris of Karlova trembled as the leaves of the aspen tremble to a breeze. Even though the whispered words were plain enough he could not believe that he had heard aright, yet there could be no mistake. Slowly he extended his arms through the grating of his cell and took the little figure of the Princess Mary in them; but as he bent his lips toward hers, the girl placed a palm across them and pushed him away.

"Not that!" she gasped. "I have sunk pride and endured shame to tell you the thing I have told you; but I am still a princess—my lips are not for you even though I love you. For your sake alone I have acknowledged my love, in the hope that because of it you would speak the truth that will save your life and mitigate the misery of mine. Promise me that if I send an officer you will tell him what you will not tell me."

Prince Boris' arms dropped to his sides. He turned back into his cell, his shoulders stooped like those of an old man.

"I cannot," he said, "for when you know, Mary of Margoth, you will hate me—I prefer death to that."

"You will not tell, then?" she asked.

He shook his head. Without another word the girl turned and walked slowly up the corridor. The man saw the door open, saw her pass through, and saw it close behind her. Then he threw himself upon the hard bench at the back of his cell and buried his face in his hands. For the first time in his life Prince Boris of Karlova knew utter misery.

CHAPTER EIGHTEEN

ALL night he sat there, and there they found him when they came just before dawn to lead him to the courtyard of the prison where the blank wall is.

At their summons he rose and shook himself, and when he stepped into the corridor between the files of soldiery his shoulders were as stiff and his chin as high as when he rode at the head of The Black Guard through the boulevards of Sovgrad. With a firm step, and a half smile upon his lips, he marched out into the chill of the early morning. An arc lamp sputtered above the courtyard close to the blank wall. He saw it and the squad of soldiers drawn up opposite, and he knew that the light was there for the purpose of revealing their target to the men.

He spoke but once as they placed him in position with his back against the wall, and that was to ask that they leave his hands free and his eyes unbandaged. Then the soldiers who had brought him from his cell stepped aside; an officer asked him if he had anything to say before his sentence was carried out. Prince Boris shook his head.

Very clearly he heard the short, sharp commands of the lieutenant in command of the firing squad. "Ready! Aim!—" Prince Boris licked his dry lips and stared very hard at the young lieutenant.

Why did the man hesitate so long before giving the final command? The prisoner saw the officer cast an uneasy glance in the direction of a door which led from the interior of the prison into the courtyard, then he saw the door open and an officer in full uniform hurry toward them. His hand was upraised, and as he came he cried aloud: "Stop! In the name of the king, stop!"

The newcomer exchanged a few words with the lieutenant, then he approached the prisoner.

"You will accompany me," he said. "His Majesty, the King, has sent for you."

Under guard Boris was conducted to the palace, up a broad staircase and along a marble corridor at the end of which were two massive doors. At these doors his guard halted, and the officer who had brought him from the courtyard and the stone wall advanced and struck upon the panels with his gloved knuckles. Instantly the doors swung inward, revealing to Prince Boris as astonishing a sight as he had ever witnessed.

A dozen officers, resplendent in showy uniforms

were grouped on either side of a table at which sat two elderly men. There was Prince Stroebel, and two other functionaries of Margoth, the prime minister of Karlova, Baron Kantchi, Boris' three cronies, Alexander, Ivan, and Nicholas; the American, Hemmington Main; General Demetrius Gregovitch, Karlovian Minister of War; and a very much frightened little girl whom Boris' astounded eyes recognized as Bakla, the barmaid of Peter's Inn. But the one which caused the prisoner the greatest surprise by his presence there was he who sat at the table beside Alexis III of Margoth. Like a man in a trance the crown prince of Karlova stood staring at the big-fisted, red-faced man who glared at him from beneath his bushy eyebrows, and who was none other than his royal sire, King Constans of Karlova.

Boris advanced to the table behind which the two rulers sat, and bowed low before them. King Constans rose and walked around the end of the table to his son's side.

"You are a damn fool," he said, and his voice was husky with emotions; "but I watched you just now from a window of the prison overlooking the courtyard. I saw you before the firing squad, and my only regret is that I haven't a dozen more damn fools for sons."

For the first time in many years Constans of Karlova put his arms about his only child and embraced his with real affection.

"I don't understand," stammered Prince Boris. "What does all this mean? How did you find out?"

"You may thank this young person," replied his father, pointing to Bakla. "She rode to Sovgrad and found Ivan—told him the fix you were in—made him come to me, by jove, and confess the whole fool thing.

"And you may thank his gracious majesty, King Alexis, and our good friend and servant Baron Kantchi for the lesson which they prepared for you and which terminuted just now before the stone wall in the prison courtyard."

"You mean that the whole thing was a hoax," exclaimed Boris, flushing—"that it was never intended that I be shot?"

"We knew who you were before that indictment and sentence were read to you," said Alexis.

"And the Princess Mary—did she know?" he asked.

"She does not know yet," replied the king of Margoth, "and I rather doubt that she would care much what became of Prince Boris of Karlova after her experience with him in Demia day before yesterday—do you?" and Alexis III scowled his fiercest scowl.

"Yes, Your Majesty, I do," blurted Prince Boris, "because she loves me and I love her."

"Then you'd better go and tell her about it, my son," said Alexis; "you'll find her in the adjoining room."

As Prince Boris crossed the threshold and closed the door behind him he found himself in a dimly lighted room on the opposite side of which a little figure crouched in a huge easy chair before a log fire.

At the sound of the opening and closing door the figure leaped to its feet and turning toward Boris cried: "What word? Have they murdered him, or have they set him free?" and then as the man crossed toward her and she saw who he was, she gave a little cry and ran toward him. "You?" she gasped.

"I, Your Highness," he replied, and going upon one knee he raised her fingers to his lips. "It is I with a confession and a plea for mercy," and then he told her.

"I can't be angry," she said, "For I didn't want to marry you any more than you wanted to marry me. How could we know, who had never seen one another, that we were born into the world, just you for me and I for you?"

It was fully half an hour before Alexis III sent Ivan Kantchi into the adjoining room to discover what had become of Prince Boris of Karlova. Though he rapped upon the door a dozen times he received no response, and so he turned the knob and entered. What he saw beyond the arm of the easy chair before the log fire sent him back into the room from which he had come.

"War is hell," he said, bowing low before the two kings, "and from what I have just seen in the adjoining room I am positive that there will never be war between Margoth and Karlova."

Hemmington Main and Gwendolyn Bass were married in Demia before they left for America.

Prince Boris of Karlova was best man and Princess Mary of Margoth maid of honor.

And what became of The Rider? I wish that I could tell you that he reformed and was pardoned by both King Alexis III and King Constans, and that he married Bakla and settled down to run a nice, respectable, little tavern on the Roman road just out of Sovgrad. Would you like to have me tell you that? All right, I will; but it isn't so.

EDGAR RICE BURROUGHS

$1.25 each

Beyond the Farthest Star

Cave Girl

Eternal Savage

The Lad And The Lion

The Land of Hidden Men

The Land Time Forgot

The Lost Continent

The Mad King

Monster Men

Moon Maid

The Moon Men

The Mucker

The Oakdale Affair

Out of Time's Abyss

Outlaw of Torn

The People Time Forgot

Return Of The Mucker

The Wizard of Venus

EDGAR RICE BURROUGHS